D1648593

MAYA NICOLE

TRANSCEND

CELESTIAL ACADEMY BOOK 3

Emily,
Forever.
Thanks for
reading! Maya Nicole

 Created with Vellum

Playlist

Cloud - Elias
In My Veins -Andrew Belle
Symmetry - SYML
At My Weakest - James Arthur
Rescue - Lauren Daigle
Birds - Imagine Dragons
Blackout - Freya Ridings
Skin - Rag'n'Bone Man
Tennessee Whiskey - Chris Stapleton
Silence - Marshmello

Author's Note

Transcend is a reverse harem romance. That means the main character will have a happily ever after with three or more men. This book also contains male/male romantic encounters, as well as several romantic encounters together as a group.

Some scenes may trigger some readers due to PTSD flashbacks, abduction, bullying, and a relationship with a teacher in a college academy setting.

Recommended for readers 18+ for adult content and language.

Chapter One

*B*reathe in. *Breathe out.*

The words played on repeat in my head as I focused on the movement of my chest. My skin felt sticky and hot. I could feel the scar knitted together on my chest as each breath stretched the scar tissue. The scar that had closed over the wound that had taken part of my heart.

It had been over a month since my mother stabbed me in the chest and then sent a hell serpent to finish the job. The hell serpent had failed. Lilith had not.

It had been over a month since she took my dad.

I desperately wanted to find him. Lilith was beyond psychotic, and the longer she had him, the worse off we would all be. No one knew where they were exactly. Hell, probably. None of the archangels wanted to go on an expedition into an unknown realm. Especially when there had been no sign of Lilith since that night.

Where else would she have taken him?

I gripped the sides of the lounge chair. *We have to find him.*

"Cannonball!" My eyes popped open behind my sunglasses as Olly ran past me and jumped into the pool. Water splashed over the sides and onto me. I jumped up from my chair.

We really needed to have a talk about mimicking movies. It was all fun and games until someone got hurt. Like he was about to.

"Damn it, Olly!" I wiped the water from my skin that had just started baking at the level I wanted it. I walked to the edge of the pool and put my hands on my hips. "You're going to pay for that!"

Asher's laugh grabbed my attention, and I looked over at him laying a towel on the chair next to mine. He had his hair pulled back in a small bun at the nape of his neck and his aviator sunglasses shielded his eyes. I'm sure they were twinkling with glee over Olly's assault.

"Did he get you all wet?" He cocked an eyebrow as he pulled his shirt off.

I bit my lip and perused his well-defined chest as he threw his shirt on the chair and pulled his sunglasses off. What was I mad about again?

"Someone got me wet." I plopped back down

on my chair and watched as Asher walked to the edge of the pool.

He looked over his shoulder at me and gave me a shit-eating grin before jumping into the pool, sending more water in my direction.

Dick.

I couldn't stop a smile from turning up my mouth. Smiling made me feel guilty, but Asher, Olly, Tobias, and Reve had made it their mission to get me smiling again.

I let out a sigh and laid back again, the moment of glee over as quickly as it began. How could I pretend to be happy when my dad was missing and so many had died?

The hell serpent might have been dead, but that wouldn't bring back the hundreds that were in its path to get to me. Media coverage of the incident had been sparse in the days following the attack.

Chinese President Calls for Investigation into Military Mishap

Shanghai, China - An investigation is underway in Shanghai, two days after an experimental drone killed 243 people and injured hundreds more. China's armed forces are taking responsibility for the jetliner-sized aircraft that malfunctioned during a test flight, entering a densely populated area of Shanghai.

Ironically, most structural damage is to the Changzheng

Hospital, which is affiliated with the military. Losses are estimated in the billions.

HOW MANY OTHER incidents had the angels been able to cover up over the years? If they could cover up a giant monster flying through the air, who knows what else they were hiding.

Water splashed over the side of the pool, ripping me from my thoughts. Asher was trying to dunk Olly under the water. When his attempts failed, they both put their arms over the side and looked up at me.

"Why don't you join us?" Olly ran a hand through his wet hair, making the brown strands stand on end. "I don't see how laying in the sun is relaxing."

"The weather is perfect for sunbathing. Besides, I jumped in a while ago." It really was perfect. Mid-eighties was excellent summer weather. I had been spending too much time indoors.

"You're going to get wrinkles," Asher teased. I watched as Olly turned towards him, grabbed him around the waist, and then flung him back into the water.

I shut my eyes again and let the sounds of Asher and Olly horsing around fade into the background. I was just starting to feel the much-needed burning sensation of the sun again when I felt the sun disappear.

I cracked an eye open to find Tobias and Reve standing above me. They both had intense expressions on their faces.

"Like I was saying, the Dodgers are taking it all the way this season." Tobias pulled off his shirt and folded it neatly. "And when they do, it'll be time to pay up."

"They'll make it to the postseason, but then choke like they usually do."

Both my eyes were open to watch the display in front of me as Reve removed his shirt. All four of them were a sight to behold when shirtless. It was like I had my very own *Magic Mike* cast. I was sure they'd have stripped if I'd asked.

I definitely needed to ask.

I still didn't quite understand how they were all mine. This summer was giving me man overload though.

"Isn't there anywhere on this damn campus where I can get some peace and quiet?" I grumbled.

I loved them, but I was sick of hearing about baseball all the damn time. Some women might join their significant others in their love of the game. I just didn't see the appeal besides it being a nice way to fall asleep quickly.

Los Angeles Celestial Academy might be situated on twenty acres, but they never strayed farther than twenty feet from me it seemed, despite there being hardly anyone on campus for the summer.

Silence met my ears and a small smile formed

on my lips as they got the hint that I wanted them to shut up about baseball. Finally, some peace.

It was short-lived.

"Reve, there's really only one solution to this problem we're having." My eyes popped open and I watched as Tobias and Reve reached over me and shook hands. "Count of three?"

I let out a shriek as their hands reached for me. I tried to scramble off the chair, but Tobias took my left side, and Reve took my right. They lifted me like I weighed nothing and walked in sync to the pool.

They needed to stop ganging up on me. Unless it was in the bedroom. I was all for that.

"I'm going to kill-" They tossed me into the pool, the water gliding over my sun-kissed skin. I sank below the surface and came up spluttering.

"What was that, Dani?" Reve laughed before jumping in. He came up and slicked his dark hair back. "Want to see a neat party trick?"

Tobias sat on the edge and dangled his feet in as I swam over to the side. "If the party trick includes kicking your asses, then sure."

I turned to face Reve, but he was gone. Or at least his body was. I could make out his head by the water droplets floating in the air. He moved towards us, the water drops moving with him. It looked like a movie special effect where the rain stopped mid-air.

If the dream demon thing stopped working for him, he could always start a career in Hollywood.

"You promised not to use any of your abilities on campus," Tobias warned. They had gotten into it several times over the past few weeks over the same issue.

Reve let out a grunt and reappeared. "There is no one here. Even if there was, how would they know if they can't see me?" He rolled his eyes and then smirked. He grabbed Tobias's legs and yanked him into the pool with us.

"Reve has a point," Olly said, appearing right next to us. "There's no one here to see anything."

He grabbed me around the waist and turned me towards him. On instinct, my legs wrapped around his waist, and I rested my arms around his neck.

"Do you think of anything else these days?" I gasped as he lifted me enough for my breasts to be out of the water. He planted a kiss right on the top of my cleavage.

"He has a one-track mind." Asher swam up behind me and put his hands on my waist and his mouth next to my ear. "And right now, this bikini is not helping."

I arched back into Asher as Olly moved his mouth to mine and parted my lips with his tongue. This was definitely my preferred way of keeping my mind off things. I wasn't going to complain about being sandwiched between two hot, wet men.

Asher's lips trailed down my neck to my shoulders as I moaned into Olly's mouth. Our tongues tangled in a hot kiss that made my skin heat more than the sun. I was surprised the water around us wasn't boiling from the amount of heat in the kiss.

"Danica, your phone is ringing," Tobias's voice snuck into my lust-filled ears where the only sound I could hear was my heart beating, not the incessant bells of my phone alarm.

"Crap," I moaned, pushing away from Olly and Asher. I swam to the pool ladder and climbed out, feeling like I weighed three times what I usually did. Leave it to gravity to remind me that I had the weight of the world on my shoulders.

I grabbed my phone and turned off the alarm. I had a meeting with Sue Whittaker to discuss my options since my guardian placement exam showed what she called "a complete incompatibility" with being a guardian angel.

I wasn't surprised. I wasn't an angel. In fact, I was precisely fifty percent angel and fifty percent demon. Despite Rafael experimenting with angel blood transfusions, it always went right back to fifty-fifty.

"Want me to go with you?" Tobias hoisted himself out of the pool and made his way towards me. I licked my lips as water droplets skated down his skin.

After toweling myself off and sliding on my shorts, I looked over at Tobias again before pulling on my tank top. His brows were drawn together. I let out a puff of air and slid my feet into my flip flops.

"It'll be fine. I don't think it's a good idea for you to poke the bear any more than you already have." I slid my phone into my back pocket and put my sunglasses on the top of my head.

"I'll go," Olly shouted from the pool. "We can hold hands the entire time. She'll love that!"

"I can go in my phantom form and mess around with her a bit." Reve sat down on my empty chair. "But that might give away that I've been the one fucking around with her shit the last few weeks."

I put my hands on my hips and looked down at him. "Michael told you to knock that off because he didn't want to have to listen to her screeching at him."

He grinned and shrugged. "That wench insulted all of us. Plus, she's taking out all of her insecurities on poor Tobias here. Think of it as repentance for her sins. If it makes it easier."

When we had returned from Shanghai, Michael sequestered me to the campus. As unhappy as I had been, the dean had been even more so. Sue had been livid with having not only me back but also Tobias and Asher. To top it off, Michael had given special permission to Reve to be on campus.

I had thought Sue's head was going to explode with how red she turned at the news that a demon would be staying until further notice.

"I'm sure I can handle myself. If I can survive a knife to the chest, I think I can survive a tongue lashing from a bitter old woman." I touched my scar through my shirt and plastered a smile on my face. "Be ready with alcohol and pizza, just in case."

I made my way across campus to Ariel Hall and up to the second-floor administrative offices. It would have been faster to get a ride with one of the guys, but sometimes it was good to walk instead of flying everywhere.

It was quiet since there were only a few staff members on campus for the summer. I turned the corner leading to the dean's office and nearly collided with a mountain of a man with long blond hair. Michael had a phone plastered to his ear and a pensive look on his face. He held up his hand in silent greeting before stalking back down the hall.

The dean's office door was closed, so I sat in one of the chairs outside the door and watched Michael pace back and forth down the hall.

I felt sick. If the archangel was here, it couldn't be good. The meeting was supposed to be just Dean Whittaker and me.

"Next time, please try not to kill them... Well, obviously if it is spitting fire, kill those... You should be able to handle one of those, Ham... They torture souls, so what if we torture them?... Don't give me a lecture about my moral compass!" He ended the call and then turned to look at me. "Sorry about that. Chamuel can be a pill."

I nodded. Anytime Michael was around, I felt like I was in the presence of a major celebrity and could hardly find words. It might also have been the fact that he was one scary-ass angel that looked like he could remove someone's head with his bare hands.

"More demon attacks?" I managed to ask as he raised his fist and knocked on Sue's door.

I stood as he opened the door to the office. He looked back at me and gave me a curt nod.

Demons had been coming through the barrier to Earth more and more frequently over the last month. Usually, it was only a few and nothing like the attack at the abandoned mall. Still, demons coming to Earth had disaster written all over it.

Just ask the two hundred and forty-three people who died in Shanghai.

"Michael, what a pleasant surprise," Sue said as we walked into her office. She didn't sound like it was a pleasant surprise at all.

"Well, as you know, I receive notifications of all meetings and interactions logged in the system for Danica now." He sat down in a chair and crossed his legs. "So imagine my surprise when I get a notification on my phone that you've scheduled a meeting without my consent or notifying me personally."

Sue opened her mouth to speak, but Michael held up his hand. She sat down in her chair and moved some papers around on her desk. I took a seat next to Michael.

What was he, my Heaven-appointed advocate now?

"You said you want to speak to me about incompatibility with being a guardian angel?" I couldn't help but smile as she shifted uncomfortably in her seat.

She let out a strained laugh and pulled out a sheet of paper. "Well, yes. It seems your test results yielded no results for the four guardian angel paths we have here."

"Oliver doesn't have a path, either." I folded my hands in my lap. He was an archangel. All the paths were his. "I will just take whatever classes he is taking."

"Oliver Morgan is an archangel, Ms. Deville. This is hardly the same thing. It will be rather difficult for you to participate in the Advanced Healing Techniques course when you have no healing powers."

She looked at Michael to gauge his reaction. He sat silently next to me. She took his silence as permission to continue.

She looked back at me and picked up her pen. "You are not an angel. It's time for us to all acknowledge that your attendance here is at a detriment to angels who earned the right to call themselves guardian angels."

I looked over at Michael, who looked bored

with this entire exchange. Shouldn't he be saying something? It was his idea for me to stay here in the first place. No wonder Lucifer didn't like him. My dad would never let someone speak to me the way Sue was.

"Earned their right? Maybe at some point they did. I think you're fooling yourself if you think some of the students here are any better than I am." I crossed my arms over my chest. "Besides, I'm half-angel. My blood tests confirm that."

She didn't need to know that the other half was demon or that my mother was Lilith. If she knew, the entire academy would know. I could only imagine the torment that would happen if that piece of information came out.

She made a strangled noise in her throat. "Even so, you have no abilities. Not to mention the company you seem to keep. Angels do not befriend or date demons. Him being on campus poses great danger to us all. It's bad enough it's being requested that Tobias Armstrong stay here when he's been suspended. Don't even get me started on that Fallen drunk that walks around half-dressed."

I wanted to laugh but bit my inner cheek. I couldn't deny the fact that Asher drank too much. He also had the tendency to walk around without a shirt. It didn't help that one day, Sue had entered the staff building and found him naked on the common room couch.

That had gone over *real* well.

A silence fell over the room. I willed myself to not break eye contact with the woman who had hated me before she had even known me. Her pen started to tap as the silence in the room lengthened.

"Sue." Michael cleared his throat. "Were you aware that Danica visited the white room?"

Michael had his eyes locked on Sue. She bristled at the mention of the room I had woken up in while dying of a stab wound. I was only half-surprised that Michael knew I had been knocking on Heaven's diamond-encrusted door.

It just wouldn't open for me.

"But how? There are only two ways for a person to get out of that room." Her pen dropped to the desk. She looked back and forth between us. I furrowed my brows because there had just been one door. Plus swirling. Lots and lots of swirling. "By going to Heaven or going to hell."

"It seems there are more important things in store for Danica. We don't know exactly what yet, but when the time comes, we want her as prepared as possible. You will enroll her in the warrior courses." He stood and crossed his arms. "And Sue? Need I remind you that you are easily replaceable. I can think of one perfectly suitable candidate that is unoccupied this next semester. I'm sure he would be willing to pick up the slack."

Her jaw nearly hit her desk. I stood and followed Michael out of the office. I looked back at

Sue and gave her a sticky sweet smile before shutting the door.

"What exactly does being a warrior entail?" Sure, I could throw a punch, but being some kind of fighter?

"Hard work." He turned and put his hands on my shoulders. It was a very fatherly move, and my eyes teared up as he looked down at me. "Hard work and passion."

"Do you think we'll find him?" I broke eye contact with him and stared at the center of his chest.

He sighed. "We will."

"Do you think he'll be okay?" I looked back up again and saw sadness in his eyes. He let go of my shoulders.

"He'll live." His phone vibrated in his pocket, but he didn't move to answer it. "We are getting closer to finding him. We'd be closer if Chamuel stopped killing the demons we can get information from."

He'd live. That didn't ease the dread swirling in my gut. He'd live, but he probably would never be the same.

Chapter Two

*J*une had come and gone. With nothing but an empty campus and time on my hands, I had already caught up on the coursework from the first semester that I hadn't been in attendance. I had also been working on perfecting my cooking skills in the large academy kitchen.

Me. Danica Marie Deville. Cooking. It was newsworthy and should have been taken to the press. They'd have a field day and warn the masses of impending doom.

The campus had taken on a whole new look and feel with it empty. I had always been so focused on avoiding the haters that I had never stopped to appreciate its beauty or what it had to offer. I hadn't even known there was a pool or state of the art fitness facility.

Not that I used the fitness facility. Although, maybe I should since I was a warrior now. The idea made me laugh.

I jumped onto the stainless-steel workstation in the kitchen and pulled out my phone. Tobias was supposed to be teaching me how to make pasta from scratch. *Where are you?*

Sorry! On my way, there was an extra inning.

I rolled my eyes and pulled up a list of ingredients for pasta. It seemed easy enough. If I messed it up and it tasted like cardboard, I would just blame Tobias and his baseball obsession.

I slid off the counter and pulled out the flour, eggs, and olive oil. It would have been easier to just use boxed pasta, but Tobias insisted on fresh since we had use of an actual kitchen.

I missed my own kitchen. Not that I had used it much, but the few times I did cook in it, the food had been a hit. Or at least I thought it was. No one had died.

The kitchen door swung open. Tobias rushed in, out of breath. He was dressed in jeans, a Dodgers shirt, and a backward baseball cap. I'd much rather have had him for dinner.

"Did they at least win?" I asked as he came around the counter. He stepped behind me and wrapped his arms around my waist.

"Of course they won." He kissed my neck, his beard tickling the sensitive skin below my ear. I tilted my head to the side and shut my eyes as he peppered kisses across my neck. "You ready?"

"I'm always ready," I breathed. Tobias chuckled and stepped around me to lean against the counter. "Oh, you meant to make pasta."

"What else would I have been talking about?" He opened a cabinet and pulled out a pasta maker contraption. It looked like some kind of medieval torture device.

"I'll remember that later." I hip bumped him as he grabbed the measuring cup I was holding out of my hand and dumped a pile of flour on the counter. "The recipe says-"

"Pasta making is an art form. Recipes are for noobs." He grabbed a second type of flour from the pantry and dumped it on top of the pile. "I'm no noob."

"You aren't Italian, are you?"

"My best friend growing up was Italian." He created a well to act as a bowl for the eggs in the center of the flour. "Want to crack four eggs in the center?"

We fell into a comfortable silence as we made the pasta and started the sauce. I popped a pan of meatballs in the oven and turned to find Tobias watching me.

"Were you checking out my ass?" I pulled him into a hug, burying my face in his shirt. He wrapped his arms around me, and his hand ran up and down my spine.

"Just worrying, as usual," he said into my hair. "I can't help it."

"I'm fine." I pulled back slightly so I could look at him. "What's there to worry about?"

He pushed a lock of hair out of my face and behind my ear, leaving his hand on the side of my neck. His thumb stroked my jaw. I shut my eyes and sighed.

"What if I somehow manipulated you into falling in love with me?" I whispered. It had been on my mind for weeks.

His thumb stilled for a moment before continuing to stroke in soothing swipes across my skin.

"I don't think that's possible. My love runs pretty deep." His thumb brushed over my bottom lip. "You aren't your mother."

I pulled away from him and went to the stove, checking on the sauce. I stirred it for longer than necessary before turning back to him.

"I am, though. At least fifty percent of me." I turned off the burner and put a lid on the pan. "I can manipulate demons and humans. It wouldn't be such a stretch to think that I had somehow coerced you guys into being with me. I mean, there *are* four of you. That's a bit abnormal." I crossed my arms over my chest and leaned against the opposite counter.

We had talked about my newly discovered ability after returning from China but hadn't discussed it as much as we should have. Every time I was around them, I wondered if I had somehow duped them into being with me.

"Let's test it." He placed his arms on either side of me, trapping me against the counter. "Make me bark like a dog or kiss your feet."

His eyes danced in amusement. I didn't think it was funny that everything I thought we had might be one-sided. I did want to test it, but the thought made me want to throw up. What if he barked like a dog?

"You don't need anything else to worry about. Just give it a try so it'll be one less thing to think about." He stepped back. "I'm ready."

I sighed and stood up straight. I balled my fists at my side, which somehow helped. If I had been somehow controlling them all, what would we do? Would they leave me?

"Bark like a dog." Nothing. "Tobias, bark like a dog."

"Is this some kind of new sex foreplay you two are into?" Reve's voice came from the doorway just before the door opened. Olly and Asher walked in. "If so, I'm not sure I'm going to be into it."

"Kitchen foreplay? That sounds like fun. Where's the whipped cream?" Asher went to the stove and lifted the lid. "It smells good in here. What's on the menu besides foreplay?"

"Danica thinks she made us fall in love with her." Tobias kissed my cheek in reassurance.

"Well, she kind of did, didn't she? I mean, I'm in love with her. I don't know about you fools." Asher pulled me in for a kiss before passing me off to Olly, who did the same.

Reve appeared and took my hand, kissing the top of it like a gallant suitor from a different century. My heart fluttered and my face flushed.

My heart always felt unstable when all four were around me.

"Show off," Tobias coughed into his hand. "What I meant was, she thinks she can control us like Lilith can control demons."

Reve paled and cleared his throat. "You think you forced us into this?" He shook his head. "It doesn't feel like it. When someone is controlling you, you feel it right here." He put his hand over my chest, right over my heart. "It's like someone is pulling strings and constricting the blood flow."

The timer for the meatballs went off, saving me from the uncomfortable conversation. I pulled them out of the oven, and the scent of meaty goodness filled the air. My stomach growled, despite the knot that sat in it.

"Maybe Tobias is right. I should test it out on all of you. After we eat. I'm starved."

After making our plates, we headed out to the empty dining room. There was a circular table that was the perfect size for the five of us and gave a view to the outside courtyard.

"I have to go check in on my guys tomorrow. We're almost finished with a refurb, and I need to make sure they haven't fucked up my design." Asher took a drink of his wine. "So, if you need anything from your place, just text me a list and where to find it."

I sighed. I hated not being able to be at my apartment. I had barely even moved in before shit hit the fan with Lilith. Now I was sequestered back where I was trying to escape from. "I still don't see why I can't go home. Tobias can just suppress my aura or whatever it is you can do."

"I could, but we aren't going to take that chance. That hell serpent still found you, and I was actively hiding you. It could be the demon side of you."

I nearly choked on a meatball. We didn't often talk about me being a demon. Mostly because it made me freak out and cry. I was still waiting for the day I sprouted an extra head or grew tentacles.

"It might be good to test things out. If demons come our way, we can just fly back here. I know Michael said to stay here, but it's my birthday." Olly shoved half a meatball into his mouth and made a noise of approval. His days of eating the same foods were long gone.

"What do you mean it's your *birthday*?" Asher put his fork down and folded his arms on the table. "*Tomorrow* is your birthday?"

Olly shrugged. "I kind of forgot about it until earlier today. I don't know the exact date, but it was before July Fourth."

"Angel baby, you can't just spring something like this on us on such short notice. This is your first birthday!" Asher finished his wine and reached for the bottle to pour himself more. Olly watched him with raised eyebrows. "Don't give me that look. I've had one glass tonight."

"I didn't say anything." Olly's voice was monotone.

I frowned at their tense exchange. Now that we practically all lived together, Asher's drinking problem had become glaringly obvious. Olly was the most vocal about it.

"Are you finally cutting back?" Tobias set his fork down and let out a content sigh as he leaned back in his chair.

"Trying to, but then my boyfriend drops surprise birthday news. Now I'm forced to have another glass." He filled his glass and took a drink from the bottle. "And don't start." He pointed the top of the bottle at Reve.

Reve held up his hands before grinning at the two of them. He was an instigator and liked to stir the pot as much as possible. He didn't sleep and had too much time on his hands to plot.

"I wasn't going to say anything." Reve stood and walked over to the window overlooking a courtyard.

"I'm just glad he dropped birthday news and not a bar of soap. Some things I do *not* want to see."

I threw my head back and laughed along with Tobias as Asher jumped up from the table and darted towards Reve. Reve disappeared but started whistling as he moved around the dining room.

"You filthy son of a bitch. It's a good thing you don't sleep." Asher swatted at the air where the laughing was coming from. "Or you'd need to sleep with one eye open."

Reve reappeared, sitting cross-legged on a table on the other side of the room. "Is that a threat, angel? Because if it is, *you* do sleep."

"Can't we all just get along?" Olly rested his cheek on his fist. "Why would I have a bar of soap at dinner, anyway? Sometimes you make absolutely no sense."

"Maybe next time you two shower together, Asher can drop a bar of soap and show you what I was referring to." Reve climbed off the table after Asher returned to his seat.

"We have to do something off-campus for his birthday. I vote we go on a field trip tomorrow," I said, returning their attention back to what we had been discussing. The mental image of them in the shower was still playing on repeat in my head.

"It's not worth the risk." Tobias sighed and ran a hand over his beard.

"I'm with Dani on this one. We can't just keep

her here indefinitely. There's three of us that can fly her back here if we need to." Asher looked over at Olly, who nodded in agreement.

"Fine." Tobias stood and started stacking plates. I was surprised he was clearing off the table. "But don't say I didn't warn you."

After cleaning up our dinner mess, we headed to the gymnasium to test my theory about controlling them. Tobias was immune, but the others might not be.

The gymnasium was the safest place to test out my ability without the risk of prying eyes seeing us. The campus was mostly empty, but Sue Whittaker was on campus at times, and so were a few other teachers who were on rotation to keep the wards intact.

"So, how are we going to do this? Are you just going to tell us to do shit and then see if we do it?" Asher had his arms folded across his chest. "Wouldn't this be more interesting done in a bedroom?"

"Are you always such a horny bastard?" Reve had his hands shoved in the pockets of his jeans. He looked nervous. I can't say I blamed him since the last time someone commanded him to do something, it was meant to kill him.

We hadn't talked about that night in Shanghai when Lilith had told him to give visions to a crowd full of people. He had tried resisting her request but had done her bidding. Tobias had flown him away before he had drained himself completely.

None of us knew what Reve was fully capable of. Apparently, being a dream demon didn't just mean he could invade a person's dreams. He could send terrifying images while a person was awake.

"If you two don't knock it off, I'm going to make you sit with your arms around each other," Tobias warned. At times, the fatherly side of him came out. Dealing with the three other men did feel like wrangling a group of unruly children.

I was a handful myself.

I stood in front of Asher. He used to be Fallen, and I wondered if at first, I had swayed his opinion of me. He had been a notorious womanizer before meeting me, or at least that's what I assumed from the stories he shared.

"Fly." He raised his eyebrows at my command, but stayed in front of me. I tried a few other commands, but he stood firmly in place, a smug look on his face.

"See. No fake love here." He leaned forward and kissed me.

I tried Olly next, who yielded the same results. Maybe I was overthinking everything that had happened in Shanghai. These men loved me without strings attached. I knew that deep in my heart, but I'm sure my dad also felt some things deep in his heart for Lilith. Look how that turned out.

I stood in front of Reve. His eyes were wider than usual. He looked to be in pain. Not the physical kind, but the kind that ripped your heart to shreds. I brought my hand to his face.

"I'm going to do whatever you tell me to do. I can tell you for certain that you didn't brainwash me into falling in love with you." He spoke so only I could hear him. There was an edge to his voice like he was holding back what he really wanted to say.

I searched his eyes, trying to understand how he was feeling. Reve might have been the newest addition to my group of guardians, but he was the one I had come to rely on the most. Without him, I'd have been walking around like a zombie.

"Kiss me." He complied, taking my lips with his. His lips trembled against mine before pulling away.

I took a sharp inhale of air. I didn't want to start questioning every single thing between us.

His hands fell to his sides, and he backed up a few steps. "Something other than kiss you or touch you. It's not like I can resist that command."

I sucked my bottom lip in between my teeth to keep the whimper in my throat from coming out. Tobias stepped forward to stand beside me, placing his hand on my lower back.

"Do a backflip." He nodded. I watched in fascination and sadness as he landed a perfect backflip.

"Again."

"Reve, we don't-"

"Again."

"Lay on the floor."

As Reve laid down on the floor, Asher stood on the other side of me. "Have him do something ridiculous like waddle like a duck or crawl around like a dog."

Reve stood and glared at Asher, clenching and unclenching his fists. "I know that you walk around drunk half the time, but you do realize that I was controlled by Lilith for centuries, don't you?"

A silence fell over the gym as they stared each other down. Asher finally broke the silence. "I didn't know besides that one time. We don't read minds, Reve."

Reve ran a hand through his hair and then shook his head. "This was a shitty idea. I'm going back to the room."

We followed him out of the gym in silence. I knew Lilith had controlled him, but not that it had lasted centuries. Not that any time under Lilith's control would have been a good thing.

Once back at our building, Reve sat down heavily on the leather couch in the common room. He grabbed the television remote from the coffee table and turned on the television. I sat down next to him with the rest of the guys spreading out on other couches.

The common room was quickly becoming one of my favorite places on campus. The tall ceilings, stone fireplace, and comfortable couches made it feel like the lodge of a ski resort.

The building was empty, with the few other staff members opting to stay in a different building because of Reve. It would have pissed me off, but it ended up working out because we had privacy.

The giant flat-screen television came to life, and Reve started flipping through the endless list of movies we had on the 'to be watched' list.

"When I was younger, in my teenage years by demon standards, I snuck out one night to smoke in the woods next to our castle." Reve's eyes didn't leave the television screen, but all four of us had our eyes glued on him as he spoke. "To smoke the Inferna equivalent of what weed is here on Earth. I took my guard, Alaric, who was more of my best friend than anyone that would enforce my parents' rules. The Black Woods weren't dangerous at the time, but there were definitely stories the elders liked to tell about children being kidnapped, men being gutted, and women being taken." He sighed and put the remote on the arm of the couch. He stared off into space as if he remembered the night perfectly.

"Ric and I met up with a few buddies from the village next to the castle, and we settled into this little clearing in the trees. They came out of nowhere, the vampire demons."

"Vampires?" I took his hand, and he squeezed it tightly. There had been no mention of vampire demons in any of the books I'd read. "Blood-sucking vampires?"

"What else would they drink?" He shrugged. "I was grabbed as soon as we were aware of them. I hadn't developed my phantom form yet, so I couldn't get away."

There was a solid minute of silence before he continued. "We were outnumbered. My two other friends were killed instantly. Ric ran off into the woods with his tail between his legs."

"I'm sorry." I stroked the side of our clasped hands with my thumb. He still didn't make eye contact.

"Then, she appeared. She was the most gorgeous woman I had ever laid eyes on at the time. I stopped fighting to get away because I was so enamored by her. The vampires held me. She just walked right up to me and told me to go kill my parents and then chain myself in our dungeons."

A tear slid down my cheek as I looked down at his wrist, tattooed with a chain.

"So I killed them. I tried to stop myself, because even when Lilith is controlling you, you still have an awareness of what you're doing." He let out a shaky breath and ran a hand over his face. He shut his eyes and pinched the bridge of his nose.

I had so many questions, but the pain in his voice and face stopped me from asking them. I put my hand on his arm and squeezed.

"Why would she want you to kill your parents?" Olly was sitting on the edge of his seat and leaning forward slightly.

Reve let out a sharp laugh before standing. "She wanted the throne."

Then, he disappeared and left us to pick our jaws up off the floor.

Chapter Three

Oliver

*B*irthdays seemed to be a big deal on Earth, at least to those still alive. I was an adult who had never had a birthday. Never felt the swirl of excitement in my belly over what the day had in store for me. I hadn't thought it would be a big deal to just skip it, but no one else felt that way.

After Reve revealed he was the prince of hell the night before, we had tried to occupy ourselves with making birthday plans. I wasn't a hundred percent sure of when my birthday was. The days all blended together in Heaven. What I did know was that it was in July but before the Fourth of July.

Asher decided we needed to celebrate for three days to ensure we had the right day. I wasn't going to complain if the people I loved wanted to put all of their attention on me for seventy-two hours.

I lengthened my body under the covers, letting out a small moan as I stretched from a restful sleep. My hand fell on the empty spot next to me. Asher had to check in with his business and left before the sun had even peeked over the horizon.

The five of us had fallen into a comfortable living arrangement considering we were holed up at the academy. Most nights Asher and I slept in Tobias's room while he and Reve slept in Danica's room. Well, at least, Tobias slept.

We had talked about moving two beds into one room, but even I knew that too much testosterone in one small space would spell disaster. Danica loved us, but being around us twenty-four seven had to be a lot at times.

Especially when Reve decided to stir up drama. It kept things lively, to say the least.

I sat up, and my eyes quickly adjusted to the darkened room. Dark blobs floated around the ceiling. I switched on the lamp.

Balloons of various colors floated around the ceiling with a giant 'happy birthday' balloon tied to the back of a chair. How they had even managed to get balloons in the room without waking me up was a mystery.

There was a cupcake that sat on the table with a '1' candle on the top. I grabbed the card next to it and opened it.

Happy birthday, angel baby! Sorry, I couldn't be there for your birthday blowjob. I'll make it up to you later.

I grinned and set the card down. I would definitely collect on that later.

I was one lucky angel. After Shanghai, Asher and I decided that there was too much uncertainty to not embrace what had developed between us. We both were still crazy about Danica, but now we were also crazy about each other.

Still not crazy enough to go all the way with each other, though. I wanted it more than anything. I always thought about it, which was probably why I walked around with a hard-on most of the time now.

I got dressed and made my way to Danica's room. Some nights she would sleep with me and Asher, but until we had a bigger space or it was safe to sleep off-campus, we had to be okay with separate beds.

Reve was sitting on the floor outside the door with his back against the wall. His knees were drawn up to his chest. I put my hand on the doorknob but then backed up a few steps to look at him.

"What's wrong?" He looked distant and tired. Reve never looked tired.

It was a loaded question given what he had shared with us the night before. Everything was not right with Reve. Did he even have a last name? There were so many things we still didn't know about the demon. Thinking back on our interactions, I realized most centered around Danica. Never about him as a demon.

He was the type of demon that survived on the pain and fear he caused others. Or recently, the joy and pleasure he brought Danica in her sleep. No one wanted to admit it, but that was deep fucking soulmate level shit.

Shit. Now my thoughts were starting to sound like Asher too.

"Last night brought up a lot of memories." His voice held no emotion.

I sat down on the other side of him. Reve was the hardest one in our group to get along with. Not because he was a bad person, but he was the new guy. Plus, I think all of us were envious of his relationship with Danica.

We didn't mind sharing, but he got her all to himself for hours with no interruptions. They at least didn't rub our faces in their dream galivanting. Although I did make Danica tell me the hot air balloon dream in which he had eaten her out high up in the sky.

How did he even come up with such romantic gestures? My romantic ideas were about as creative as my pinky toe.

"Do you want to talk about it?" I touched his arm and sent a wave of calmness to him. I hadn't tried anything with him yet. I didn't even know if my abilities would work on a demon.

He looked down at my hand that was covering a tattoo of a wolf and then looked up at me. He sighed and put his head against the wall.

"No wonder Asher fell in love with you." He shut his eyes. If I didn't know he didn't sleep, I would have thought he had fallen asleep. His breaths evened out, and his face relaxed. "No offense, but you're not my type."

I moved my hand from his arm. "Why do you always have to be like that?"

"Be like what?" One of his eyes popped open. He looked back at me before shutting it again. "I'm just letting you know."

"Make everything some kind of joke."

"When you've lived for as long as me and have done the things I have, finding a way to laugh is the only way to stop yourself from self-destructing. Asher is the same way."

I grunted and stood up. It was different coming from Reve.

"Well, if you need to talk or need me to send some good vibes your way, let me know." I stepped around him and turned the doorknob, cracking the door open.

"Olly." I looked down at him, his eyes still shut. "Happy birthday."

I walked into Danica's room and shut the door gently behind me. She and Tobias were still asleep.

I slipped my shoes off and slid in next to Danica. Tobias must have been awake because he moved his arms from around her, and I slid mine into place.

"Mmm." She turned over so that her head was

in the crook of my neck. "Good morning, birthday boy."

Her hand slid around to my ass and gave it a squeeze. We really needed to resolve our sleeping situation so I could wake up with her squeezing my ass daily. She slipped her hand into my back pocket.

"Is there such a thing as a birthday blowjob?" I whispered over Danica's head to Tobias, who was staring right at me.

Danica made a noise and pinched my cheek through my jeans. "Let me guess, Asher told you there was? There's birthday sex. Can't say I've ever heard of a birthday blowjob. I wouldn't be opposed to there being such a thing. January needs to hurry up and get here."

Tobias slid out of bed, and his bare ass greeted me. He did have a pretty spectacular ass.

"I'll let you two have a few minutes. That's all it'll take, right?" He chuckled as he pulled on a pair of athletic shorts and turned to smirk at me.

I frowned at him. I lasted way longer than a few minutes. In fact, I had more stamina than all three of them. Archangel perk.

"Don't be mean to the birthday boy," Danica said, removing her hand from my back pocket and unbuttoning my jeans. My dick instantly sprang to life, straining against the zipper she had yet to unzip.

"Did you see Reve?" Tobias pulled on a shirt

and grabbed a can of some coffee beverage from the refrigerator.

"He's in the hall. He isn't in the best of moods." I was having a hard time with my words since Danica had unzipped my pants and reached her hand inside to stroke me through my boxers.

"I'm going to the gym. You two have fun." He shut the door behind himself, and I let out the moan I had been holding in.

"I'm surprised... oh God, Dani. Don't stop." I rolled onto my back and tugged my pants down to my thighs.

"Surprised?" Her hand slipped into my boxers, and her fingers wrapped around my length. Her other hand slid my shirt up so she could kiss my stomach.

Surprised? What was I going to say? "Surprised he didn't stay to watch."

She laughed against my stomach, the sound the best birthday present she could give me. Seeing her happy again was the only thing I wanted.

I WAS an advocate for birthday blowjobs. I had tried to reciprocate, but Danica said there'd be time for that later. The day was about me.

We spent the morning hanging out and then took one of the academy's SUVs into the city. Tobias was on edge, but I knew if something did happen while we were off-campus, we'd be able to protect Danica.

I was practically bouncing off the walls with excitement as we waited on Asher to get home. We were on his rooftop deck under the shade of the gazebo. Reve had decided I needed to learn to play poker.

"How are you so good at this game already?" Reve complained as I gathered the chips in the center of the table and arranged them in front of me.

I shrugged and watched Tobias shuffle the cards. I wasn't about to tell them that I could see their cards. Not when the mention of strip poker in the future was on the table.

Danica narrowed her eyes at me; I couldn't stop the smile that spread across my face. So much for having a poker face.

"You're cheating." She picked up the cards Tobias had put in front of her, glanced at them quickly and put them face down. It was cute that she thought that would stop me from seeing them.

I had tried not to see through the cards, but my brain couldn't help itself.

"I'm not. Maybe I am just really that good."

We played until Asher came home. I purposely lost a few hands just to keep things interesting. Maybe a trip to Vegas was in the near future.

We headed to the bowling alley that I had decided on the night before. Danica had a list in her phone that she added to often. It had to have at least a hundred experiences on it by now. All of which she said were necessary.

I don't know if playing hide and go seek was a necessity, but I wasn't about to argue with her.

The bowling alley was noisy, with blaring music and the sounds of balls knocking down pins. I looked over at Asher as we waited in line to borrow shoes and pay for our games. Every so often, he would flinch. I took his hand.

"Just got to get used to the sound." I squeezed his hand in reply. His eyes darted around, taking in the surroundings. He zeroed in on the bar. "Get me a size ten. You guys want anything from the bar?"

There appeared to be waitresses walking around with drink orders, but his need to escape was written clearly on his face. I let his hand go and watched him walk quickly towards the bar area.

Danica stepped up beside me and looped her arm through mine. "You worry about him too much."

"I worry about a lot of things too much," I said, looking down at her. I was worried about her. Worried about Lucifer. Worried about Reve. Even Tobias had been looking worse for wear lately.

"Remember that you need to take care of yourself too." She rubbed my arm, and we stepped up to the counter.

I didn't want to deal with my own issues. Taking care of everyone else and making sure they weren't losing their minds helped me keep my mind off of the fact that everything was my fault.

I lost the Holy Grail.

Lilith wanted it.

She got what she wanted, and in the process almost killed her own daughter and Reve. And now Lucifer was missing.

We grabbed our shoes and went to our lane. I scrunched my nose at the shoes before sliding my feet into them. They smelled like other people's feet, which made me want to gag. I saw the guy at the counter spraying shoes people brought back, but that didn't help ease my mind any.

Asher was back with a glass of something dark brown. It was most likely whiskey, his drink of choice. I thought it tasted like battery acid.

"Let's go find our balls." Asher snorted and took a sip of his drink.

"I think the blue ones are just the right weight for you three." Reve was already holding a purple bowling ball. He put it in the ball rack.

"The only person whose balls will be blue tonight will be yours when I hand your ass to you." Tobias took off in search of a ball, a cocky grin on his face.

"He must really be good at handling balls," Asher said, chuckling and taking my hand.

We followed Tobias, and all three of us ended up with blue balls after all.

After the first few frames, the rivalry between

Reve and Tobias became a sideshow. Both had only bowled strikes so far.

Reve lined himself up in front of the lane and stepped forward to release the ball.

"Gutter ball!" Tobias yelled right before he released it, causing Reve to curse as it stayed on course, but split the pins.

"Your victory is going to be marred by foul play." Reve waited for the pins to reset and his ball to return.

He couldn't knock both pins down and cursed as he returned to his seat. When it was Tobias's turn, Reve grinned. He was up to something, as usual.

"Oh. My. God. Is that Justin Timberlake?" A girl shrieked from halfway across the bowling alley. We all turned in her direction to see several women making their way toward us.

Tobias was oblivious as he stood on the hardwood and set himself up to bowl another strike. I watched in sheer fascination as the small group of women entered into our area and walked right up to Tobias, who was already bringing his arm forward. He didn't look anything like the pop star.

There's a reason you're supposed to wait for the player on the lane next to you to throw their ball. Tobias released it, which made a thud on the lane and rolled into the gutter.

"Can we get a selfie? I can't believe this is happening! Where's your wife? Are these your friends? I can't believe I'm meeting you!" The questions and comments were fired off at him as they pulled out their phones.

"What? I look nothing like Timberlake." Tobias backed up and then turned to glare at Reve. "You! I'm going to kill you!"

I was slightly surprised that Reve would send a vision, but I guess it was harmless. It made me wonder how often he used that ability.

After a lot of back and forth between Reve and Tobias, we took a break and ordered food. I wasn't too sure about eating greasy food from the bowling alley, but Danica said it was the best.

"What are we going to do for the Fourth of July?" Danica asked while we waited for our burgers to arrive. "Fireworks are out, right?"

Asher grunted and finished his second drink of the evening. "I'm glad I can come on campus now. There aren't any fireworks in the area, are there?"

"Nope. We can watch them from the top of Ariel Hall, without the loud noise."

"My dad's favorite holiday was... is July Fourth. He liked to light shit on fire," Danica said softly. She looked down at the table and then swiped at her eyes.

My breath caught in my throat. She hurt because of me. Because I was an idiot that thought trying to turn ocean water into wine was a good way to pass the time.

I stood and headed in the direction of the bathrooms. I slammed open the door and braced my hands on the counter. My heart was racing. I shut my eyes and tried to catch my breath. It felt like I had just sprinted.

The door opened behind me, and I looked in the mirror, seeing Asher slip in. He flipped the lock on the door and stepped towards me.

I straightened and turned to face him. "I don't want to talk about it."

"From the looks of it, you do need to talk about it." He leaned against the counter. "What's eating at you, Oliver?"

I put my hands in my hair, clenching the strands in my fists. "This is my fault."

He grunted and stepped towards me, grabbing my arms and pulling them until my hands were in his. "This isn't your fault."

"But I-" He shut me up with his mouth. I moaned into it before shoving him away. "Not everything can be fixed with sex."

"There's something wrong with that cup, Olly. Danica said it practically sang to her when she took it. Stop blaming yourself." Asher leaned back against the counter.

I knew all of that already, but it didn't change the fact that it had happened. I dropped it. It was safe in Heaven, and now it was with a psychotic woman who was using it for who knows what.

I doubted she was drinking wine with it.

"I don't like seeing you like this. I'm supposed to

be the deeply disturbed one, not you." Asher's face softened. He reached out a hand towards me. I took it and laced our fingers together. "Now, let's go eat. You can drown your woes in a greasy burger and a drink. I'll even throw in a wartime story."

Asher didn't talk about the war often, but when he did, it was either a hilarious anecdote or a gut-wrenching tale. I followed him back to the table where our burgers and fries were already waiting for us. My stomach growled in anticipation.

I had missed out on almost an entire year of delicious food because I didn't have the right people in my corner. Now I did, and I trusted them. So whenever they put food in front of me, I ate it. My days of cantaloupe and brown rice were over. I still couldn't resist cookies.

"This food is much better than what I got for my twenty-third birthday in 1944." Asher took the last bite of his burger and then wiped his mouth on his napkin. We all looked at him in interest. "We were on the move between towns and were eating a diet of field rations. When I came back from being on patrol, Toby here had concocted a culinary masterpiece for me. He and the guys took their biscuits from their C-Rats and ground them up, added sugar, and made a makeshift cake. They put melted lime-flavored hard candies as the frosting. Stuck a cigarette in the top and sang *Happy Birthday* to me."

"That sounds like something I'd do. How'd it

taste?" Tobias smiled at the memory he couldn't remember himself.

Asher laughed. "Like shit. I ate it though, couldn't waste precious calories." He rubbed the side of his face. "I wish I could say the rest of the day was as great as that moment, but we at least had a little fun."

"I wish I could remember some of those things," Tobias said, a wistful look passing over his eyes.

"No, you don't. For every good memory, there are ten times as many bad memories. Several members of our platoon were sniped later that day on patrol."

The table fell silent for a moment before a waitress brought out a plate with vanilla ice cream smooshed between two chocolate chip cookies.

"We ordered it for you while you were gone." Danica rubbed her hands together. "Try it."

I had tried my fair share of ice cream but never sandwiched between my favorite food. I picked it up and took a bite. If food could cause an orgasm, I would have had one.

I looked around the table at Danica, Asher, Tobias, and Reve. They were my family now, and I wouldn't trade them for anything in the world.

Chapter Four

Danica

I was not ready for classes to start. Summer had seemed to drag on forever, but as soon as the calendar rolled over to August, I didn't want it to end.

The summer brought no new news on the whereabouts of my dad. None of the captured demons knew where he was. I assumed he had to be with Lilith in Inferna, because how else were demons getting through the barrier?

I pulled my uniform out of my closet and put it on. I was going to brave the cafeteria for the sheer fact that I really had a craving for bacon.

I grabbed my bag and walked into the hall. Olly was leaning against the wall waiting for me. He grinned when he saw me. His eyes traveled down to my legs and then back up, stopping briefly on my chest before settling on my lips.

I kissed him and took his hand. Olly would be in all of my classes this semester except Weaponry since he was already skilled in that area.

It wasn't fair that he was just born one day and could wield a sword like a knight and throw daggers like a ninja. I should have been able to do at least half of those things since I was half-angel.

Things didn't quite work that way.

We made our way to the cafeteria and joined Cora and Ethan at our usual table. My eyes couldn't help but fall on the table in the corner. Several of the Divine 7 had finished the academy and moved on. It was unfortunate that Betty and Abby were still there. They saw me looking and sneered.

"I'm so excited for this year!" Cora could hardly contain her happiness. She and Ethan were doing well and had spent the summer in South America.

As much as I was opposed to being a guardian angel myself, a pang of jealousy ran through me anytime they mentioned the missions they had been on. My only mission for the summer was staying on campus. I hadn't even gotten to visit Ava. It wasn't like my best friend could come to the academy and visit me. Plus she seemed to always be working.

"I'm only excited because we have training in the evenings." Ethan slung his arm over the back of Cora's chair. "I heard there's a demon teaching us how to kill other demons."

Both Cora and Ethan looked at me. I munched on a piece of bacon. I knew what their looks were for. I was the obvious connection to the demon.

"He's a dream demon. He's decent." Olly moved his eggs around on his plate before scooping some onto his fork. He scrunched up his nose before taking a bite. "These don't taste as good as yours."

"That's because I put love in mine." I sat up a little straighter, hearing that Olly thought my cooking was better than the cooks in the back. Well, at least my eggs were.

"So this demon, how do you two know him?" Ethan asked.

"Why does everyone assume I know him because he's a demon?" I rolled my eyes.

As if on cue, Abby and her posse walked past the table, overhearing me. She stopped, several of them almost bumping into her.

"Eve, you are the spawn of Satan. Of course you'd know him. Is he one of your boyfriends now too?" A few people at the table next to us sniggered.

"Go away, Abby." Olly scooped a spoonful of oatmeal and blew on it. "No one wants to hear your nasally voice. It's ruining my appetite."

She made a noise in her throat and narrowed her eyes at him. "I see you're still slumming it with the rejects."

Olly finally looked at her and smiled. "I think you've forgotten that you were the reject back in the first semester. If I recall, you tried to cop a feel."

Her face turned red, and she opened and closed her mouth. She let out a huff and stomped off. In her previous life, she must have been a spoiled brat who threw tantrums to get what she wanted. How she became an angel was beyond my comprehension.

"Did she really?" I laughed, piling my silverware and napkin on my empty plate.

"More than once." He shrugged as Ethan gave him a fist bump. "I think she figured since the other guys let her have her way with them, that I'd be the same."

After we finished eating, we walked together to our first class: Crisis Intervention. Cora and Ethan both tested as intellectual guardian angels, but all students were required to take it.

Just like all second and third-year students were required to attend training in the evenings. You know, in case all hell broke loose.

After Crisis Intervention, which had my name written all over it, I had Weaponry without any moral support. At least it didn't involve flying.

What it did involve was Coach Ferguson and Betty. Betty didn't strike me as the type to be a warrior, but I didn't feel like a warrior myself, so I couldn't really judge.

"It's nice to see a good crop of angels for once," the coach said once class started. He paused when he saw me and raised his eyebrows. "Besides training with common weapons you might use out in the field, this evening, you will strengthen your fighting skills and swordsmanship."

Most of class time was spent with Coach Ferguson showing us different weapons: knives, clubs, tasers, handguns. I felt I was on even ground with the rest of the class for once since no one had fired a gun or wielded a taser before. At least that's what everyone said.

Betty seemed to know an awful lot about weapons.

After dinner, we were required to go to the football field for extra training. There were three rotations lasting thirty minutes each. Asher was teaching hand to hand combat with Tobias as his assistant. When Asher had shared the news, Tobias had looked furious. He was still suspended, but Michael was running the show after school hours.

Olly was with Coach Ferguson teaching swordsmanship. Despite his short time using a sword, Olly was as skilled as Michael. It must have been an archangel thing.

Then there was Reve. Reve had been all the buzz during the day, especially when word got around that he would be training us on how to kill specific demons.

I started in the group training with Asher and Tobias. Tobias was off to the side, reading a book. He wasn't taking the whole situation in his stride. Can't say I blamed him.

"Combat is no joke. When you're out there in

the trenches, anything can fucking happen. You can get a limb blown off. Lose your sight. Lose your hearing. Fucking die." Asher paced back and forth in front of us and stopped and looked right at me when he mentioned dying.

Was his speech meant to instill confidence in us? It scared the crap out of me.

"Where did they find this nut job? This isn't Vietnam," a guy behind me mumbled to another student. A few laughs broke the tension in the group.

Asher glared over my shoulder. "You're right. This isn't fucking Vietnam or World War II. This is worse. Heaven versus hell. Good versus evil. When you are staring frozen at a mother fucking Widow demon that just sent hundreds of spiders to eat your ass, are you going to be more concerned about how to kill her and her spiders or where the fuck they found this quack job?"

I cringed as he referred to himself in the third person. He wasn't helping his case any. I knew he wasn't insane but had I never met him before, I'd probably have some serious questions about him.

"This semester, we're going to push you hard because the demons are only increasing in number. We will need all hands on deck when the time comes." Tobias spoke without looking up from his book, annoyance dripping from his voice.

"The time comes for what?" Someone in the back spoke loudly, their voice shaking slightly.

"War. The apocalypse. We don't fucking know yet, but when it does happen, we'll be prepared." Asher blew his whistle for us to line up.

After running through some drills, he paired us up to practice what he called "ram and run." He paired me with Cora.

"Listen up! When I blow my whistle, partner A is going to run straight at partner B. Hit them just like we practiced, right in the midsection. Then sprint to the other set of cones."

There were lots of grumbles as we lined up on the line. I was more nervous about my lack of healing than anything else. The angels could knock each other out with no problem. I had a lot more to risk.

"Drop and give me ten burpees for that!" Fuck, he was a hardass. "You too, Danica!"

I glared at him. "I didn't complain!" I crossed my arms, and a few others joined my resistance.

"Make it twenty!" My jaw dropped. I wanted to punch him in the face. Instead, I dropped to the ground to start the burpees.

The thirty minutes seemed more like two hours. We rotated next to Olly, who was holding a pool noodle. I had only glanced in the direction of his station once when I heard the group before us laughing

I wiped the sweat from my forehead with the hem of my tank top. I had been worried about taking hits, but all along, I should have been concerned about Asher going drill sergeant on us. Tobias had just sat by, glancing up from his book occasionally, his expression unreadable

Coach Ferguson stood on a chair and blew his whistle to quiet us down. "We don't typically teach swordsmanship here at the academy since it is not common to carry a sword around on duty. A sword is the best way to incapacitate a demon long enough to take them out. Oliver will be doing most of the training with you since he is highly skilled."

I wondered how they knew a sword was best. Had demons come through before? That had to be the case.

He jumped down, and Olly took his place. "Thanks, Coach. Tonight we're going to start with our reactions to stimuli. Wielding a sword requires confidence and the ability to hold your ground, even when something is trying to take you out." He waved a pool noodle that had been cut in half in front of us. "With the same partner you just had in the last rotation, you'll act like this is a sword."

"When do we get to use a real sword?" someone in the middle shouted.

"When I feel no one is going to take someone's head off. The objective tonight is to stop your partner from hitting you with the pool noodle and to not flinch."

"This is stupid," Betty said. A few other students agreed. Betty was worse than the other six Divine combined.

"Feel free to go back to the last station since you find this activity stupid." The comment didn't even faze Olly.

After grabbing our pool noodles, Cora and I faced off.

"On guard!" I jabbed the noodle at her, and she laughed.

"This isn't fencing, Danica." She blocked me.

By the end of the half-hour, my arms were burning, My face hurt from smiling and laughing so much. Using a light object only made me realize that a real sword was going to be impossible to swing around.

Our last rotation was with Reve in a room on the side of the gym. Chairs were set up, and a projector displayed a photograph of a normal-looking man. I was pretty sure it wasn't a man. We were learning how to kill demons.

I sat in the front row with Cora and Ethan. I could feel the tension in the room as the others sat down, leaving the front row empty besides the three of us. A few teachers stood off to the sides, swords on their hips.

"Do you think they really think he's going to attack, or is it just to placate everyone?" Ethan leaned forward to ask me.

"If they are scared of a dream demon, I don't know how they expect them to fight much more frightening demons. Reve is a big teddy bear. Most of the teachers have at least been civil towards Reve. He's pretty charismatic."

Reve cleared his throat. "Let's start out with getting all of your questions out of the way. We have a lot of ground to cover, and I won't have time to answer your questions later."

Almost every hand went up except mine, Cora's, and Ethan's. Before he called on anyone, he gave a brief introduction, which eliminated about half of the hands.

"Why are you helping us?"

Reve looked at me, then at the student asking the question. "Earth has become my home. I don't think humans deserve to be terrorized by crazed demons that get through the barrier."

"Don't you terrorize humans?"

"I had a job to do here. Several of the souls I visited made it to Heaven instead of hell. The power of a well-composed nightmare is underrated."

The questioning went on for a solid fifteen minutes. Not once did Reve lose his cool or waver in his confidence. Once all questions were answered, he went on to show drawings of demons and discussed how to identify and kill them. He had drawn the pictures himself.

The time flew by, and before I knew it, the rotation was over.

"I'll see you guys tomorrow," I said, waving goodbye to Cora and Ethan.

I hung back as the room emptied. Reve was packing up his laptop.

"I think they were impressed." I tilted back in my chair and nearly fell backward. Reve laughed.

I felt my face flush and stood instead. I picked up a few water bottles left on the floor and put them in the recycling bin.

"I think they were all in shock that I didn't kill them." He slung his bag over his shoulder and led me out of the room.

It was dark outside, but the lights from the football field lit the area.

"We have a quick staff debriefing. Are you okay to walk back alone?"

"It's an angel academy, Reve." He kissed my cheek and headed off towards Ariel Hall.

I walked along the path towards the staff building. I was just about past the second student dorm building when I heard loud laughter coming from a courtyard. I moved closer to the building, so I'd be out of sight.

"Can you believe they have those idiots training us to fight demons?" One of the male Divine 7 was speaking. I couldn't remember his name, but he was a third-year, like most of them.

"Asher is fucking hot. I'd hit that. I bet he likes it rough." A girl spoke, one of the new ones.

"Gross, girl. You know that they are all in some kind of freakish relationship with devil girl, right?"

"What a slut," one of the guys said. "She's like a sex doll."

A lump formed in my throat, and I put my hand over my mouth to silence my shocked gasp. I'd talked plenty of shit about people before, but never so loudly and in such an open area.

"I think I'm going to try to hit that. Do you think she charges?"

Laughter followed.

I couldn't stop the tears from sliding down my cheeks. I should have stepped around the corner and given them a piece of my mind, but a group of assholes versus one person wasn't good odds.

I slipped around the other side of the building so they wouldn't see me and made my way towards my room.

I knew I wasn't a slut, despite what others thought. So what I was having sex with four different men? We loved each other and supported each other.

I opened my door and walked into my room, throwing my bag down and giving it a solid kick. That didn't feel like enough, so I kicked it again.

"What the hell are you doing?" Tobias popped up on the futon, running his hand over his face.

I jumped and let out a squeal.

"Aren't you supposed to be at some kind of staff meeting?" I put my hand over my heart. "Jesus, that scared me."

"Attending the staff meeting would mean I

qualified as a staff member." He laid back down. "I was only helping tonight because Asher is a little bit of a loose cannon."

I snorted. "That's an understatement."

I kicked my shoes off and walked over to the futon. I lifted his legs and sat down, putting them back down in my lap.

"You've been crying." He had his hands behind his head and was staring at me.

I patted his leg and looked at the ceiling. "I'm not just the princess of hell, Eve, or demon spawn anymore. Just call me Danica, the slutty sex doll who has four boyfriends."

"You aren't a slut." He shut his eyes. "They're just jealous."

"Being jealous isn't an excuse to sit around and talk about someone like they are an insignificant piece of trash. You know, if this was reversed and I was a man with four women, no one would say a word. If I were a boy and the son of Lucifer, everyone would think I was badass."

He snorted. "I think you're badass."

"You don't count." I looked at him and waited for him to open his eyes, but he didn't. "Are you all right?"

He sighed and opened his eyes, choosing to look at the ceiling instead of at me. I could see the worry etched on his features.

"I just want all of this to be over so we can move on with our lives. Together. Somewhere away from here." He sat up, his legs falling to the floor. "We should all just escape somewhere."

I shut my eyes as he pulled me towards him. "That would be nice."

"Somewhere tropical." He kissed my neck. "We can find an uninhabited island. Maybe build a treehouse like they did in *The Swiss Family Robinson*."

"Mmm." I tilted my head to the side, giving him better access to my neck. "Don't know who they are, but keep going."

"We can run around naked all day. Make love all night." His hand slipped under the back of my tank.

"I need a shower. I was all sweaty earlier." His lips hovered over mine. "I could use some help getting out of these clothes."

He ran his finger across the neckline of my top, sending shivers down my spine and a jolt of desire through my core.

I half expected to have steamy shower sex, but Tobias undressed me then left the bathroom to let me shower. I considered using the showerhead because he had left me hanging, but decided against it.

If Tobias wasn't in the mood, someone surely would be.

I brushed out my hair and secured the towel around my body before stepping out of the bathroom. Tobias sat shirtless on the edge of my bed, a box next to him.

"What's that?" I made my way to the bed and peeked into the box. "Holy shit."

"Reve and I stashed it under the bed. I feel like tonight is a good night to try some of it out. Might be a nice distraction for us both." Tobias reached into the box and pulled out a pair of black leather cuffs that were fuzzy on the inside. They were attached together with another piece of leather.

I clenched my thighs together as desire raced through my body. Talking about it was one thing, but knowing it was about to happen was something else entirely.

"You and Reve..." I gulped. "You bought this stuff? Together?"

I reached into the box and pulled out an eye mask and a stick with feathers on the end.

"Reve has an online shopping problem. He told me he had purchased some fun things for us to try." He moved the box off the bed and grabbed my hips, pulling me towards him.

I stepped in between his legs. "Do you two talk about sex with me or something?"

He shrugged. "Things do take a little bit of communication between the four of us. Especially since we aren't all living together." He yanked my towel, and it fell to the ground. His eyes devoured me hungrily, and he ran his hands down my sides to rest on my hips.

I gasped as he leaned forward and kissed near my belly button. "So you guys..." He pulled me to straddle his lap and trailed his lips over my breasts. "You decide who gets me when?"

He chuckled against my sensitive skin, his beard tickling. "I wouldn't put it that way. It's just better if we're all on the same page."

I jabbed my fingers through his hair as he took a nipple in his mouth, swirling his tongue around and then biting gently. They could put a schedule up on the refrigerator for all I cared.

"Dodgers," he mumbled, pulling away and looking at me. I raised my eyebrows. "That will be your safe word."

I rolled my eyes. "I don't need a safe word."

He put me on the bed and reached into the box and pulled out the cuffs, eye mask, and a pair of headphones. My eyes widened, and I held out my wrists. He laughed at my eagerness and secured them, moving them so they were on the pillow above my head.

I was shivering with anticipation as he slipped the blindfold over my eyes and then the headphones. I'd never even thought about a lack of sound during sex, but as I laid there completely incapacitated, I saw the appeal.

I could hear and feel my heart beating in my ears. He wasn't touching me yet, but somehow, I could feel his nearness on my skin. It felt as if electrical currents were jumping between our bodies.

I moaned as minutes went by. I couldn't even

tell how loud I was because I couldn't hear a damn thing.

After what felt like an eternity, I felt something on my foot. It had to be a finger trailing up from the heel. I couldn't be sure. It was soft and warm, and then hands wrapped around my ankles and pulled me down the bed.

"Tobias, you're killing me here." The only response I got was a finger trailing up my leg to my inner thigh, where it stopped and made circles.

The desire between my legs blossomed, and I slammed my thighs shut on his hand. If I could hear or see him, I bet he would have been laughing.

He pushed my legs open, and his finger was replaced by his tongue. I whimpered as it moved closer and closer to my apex. Just a little farther, and he'd be right where I wanted him.

Nothing. The fucker stopped. I let out a curse and squirmed on the covers, the fabric of the comforter soft as silk on my skin. I had never stopped to appreciate how good the sheets felt.

One side of the headphones was pulled from my ear, and a pair of lips came close. "Can I join in?"

Reve.

I nodded, words lodged in my throat. I heard both Tobias and Reve laugh as the headphones were put back in place.

I was about to orgasm at the thought of not knowing who was touching me. Would I be able to tell who was who? I would have liked to think that I would be able to tell the difference between the two men.

Hands touched my body. Mouths tasted my skin. Were they taking turns, or were both of them driving me mad with lust at the same time? They always took turns with me.

"I can't take this anymore. Please." I was desperate for something to take away the ache between my legs.

I was about to flip over and dry hump the damn sheets when a finger ran across my slit. Or at least it felt like a finger. For all I could tell, it could have been the tip of a penis. It definitely wasn't a tongue.

It worked back and forth, and then a second finger was added. They dove into my wet heat and curled against that sweet spot that made my toes curl. Over and over, the fingers brushed the sensitive place inside my pussy, driving me mad.

My body spasmed as my orgasm ripped through me like a freight train. I couldn't hear myself, but I'm sure someone standing outside would have been able to hear me.

A tongue flicked my clit, and my legs closed on instinct, the sensations of my climax still shaking my body. Could orgasms kill someone? I already felt another one about to split me in two.

A body shifted over me. The tip of a dick touched my lips, and I opened my mouth to take it inside. I slid my tongue over the head. I couldn't tell who it was. I should have been able to since they had different dicks. I needed to pay more attention.

My body trembled as he worked his length in and out of my mouth. I spread my legs, hoping whoever was unoccupied would get the hint.

Teeth scraped across my thigh, and I cried out around the cock in my mouth. A tongue ran up the length of me.

"Dodgers." I really couldn't take any more. I needed my senses back.

The headphones came off first.

"Really, you made the safe word Dodgers?" Reve's voice was amused, and as the eye mask was removed, his smiling face came into view.

After my hands were freed, I rubbed my eyes.

"You did well for your first time." Reve laid on his side next to me. He trailed a hand between my breasts and then rested it on my pubic bone.

Tobias was sitting on the end of the bed, his eyes hooded with desire. I bit my lip and looked between the two of them. Tobias never minded a little group action, but Reve had never seemed too interested.

I pushed Reve onto his back and lowered myself onto him, my thighs already quivering with the onset of another orgasm. I looked over my shoulder at Tobias, who was fisting his dick.

"I have lube in the top drawer."

His hand stopped, and his mouth opened a bit

like he wanted to say something. Instead, he stood and opened my drawer, pulling out the bottle.

Reve started moving his hips in slow rolls underneath me. I leaned forward, resting my forearms next to his head. Tobias's hand moved down my spine, and he trailed a finger between my cheeks.

I buried my face in Reve's inked neck as Tobias squirted lube on his fingers and began stretching me. I wasn't an expert in backdoor play, but after the initial shock wore off, I found myself wanting more.

His fingers left me, and the bed dipped as he positioned himself behind me.

"Relax." Reve brought his hands to my face and moved my hair behind my ears. He stopped moving underneath me as Tobias slowly worked his way into my tight hole.

"Fuck," I gasped. My entire body burned at the intrusion. It felt way better than the last time I had tried it but still was a foreign feeling.

He took it slow; his breath was strained as he held back.

"Oh, fuck," Reve moaned as Tobias began rocking his hips.

My eyes felt like they were going to roll back into my head. Reve started moving under me, matching the pace Tobias was setting. The tips of my ears and my toes felt like they had pins and needles. I felt so full and safe between them.

We should have done this sooner.

Our bodies moved together like a boat rocking gently over waves. I dug my hands into the pillow under Reve's head.

"More. Give me more," I gritted out, as my body loosened up more and what was already pretty amazing became magnificent.

Tobias grunted behind me and increased his pace. My skin was damp with sweat as our skin smacked against each other with the driving of his hips.

"Oh, God." Tobias thrust into me one last time before his body shook, and he spilled inside of me. He stayed in place as Reve dove into me harder than before.

My hand went to my clit, my orgasm mounting from what felt like fifty different directions. Tobias's hand joined mine as I pressed into it.

The orgasm, if it could even be called that because it was so much more, crashed into me with such force that I screamed out as all of my muscles seized up around Reve and Tobias.

Reve cursed and joined me, my body collapsing on top of his.

Tobias pulled out of me, the emptiness making me feel a longing to have him buried back inside me.

Reve let out a laugh and ran his fingers through my hair before gathering it over one of my shoulders. I was still lying on top of him, spent from the orgasm that went into my own personal *Guinness Book of World Records*.

"I might be old as fuck, but that was a first for me."

I slid off of him and laid on my stomach next to him. "I find that hard to believe. All those centuries and never once did you get curious?"

"Dream demons are monogamous even when dating someone. If we are lucky to find our mate, we get our strength from them."

I was about to ask him more about that when Tobias reappeared with a washcloth. He cleaned me up and then laid on the other side of me, placing his hand on the small of my back.

"Your ass okay?" He was so serious that I couldn't hold back the giggle.

"It'll be fine." I moved to lay my head on Reve's chest. "Do you think I'm your mate?"

Reve played with my hair. My eyes fluttered shut as my body relaxed.

"I think that's the only explanation. I never had the chance to ask my father and mother how it worked. My father didn't often go hunting. I just assumed he kept prisoners and fed off them."

"We should call it something else other than feeding." Tobias kissed my shoulder. "What you two have is so much more."

"We could say he eats me. That's not inaccurate."

Reve groaned and tugged my hair a little. "The

way everyone acts around you, I'm beginning to think we are all your mates. I know that's not proper human lingo, but there isn't a word for it here, is there?"

I drew a circle in the center of his chest around the tattoo of two skulls with crowns on the top of their heads. It made sense now.

"And here I thought all I was, was a sex doll."

Tobias squeezed my hip. "Stop saying that. Their opinions shouldn't matter."

"I can mess with them a bit if you want me to. Really scare the shit out of them." Reve sounded like he meant business. The allure of having him fuck with those idiots was strong.

I shook my head. As much as I wanted Reve to screw with them, I didn't want him to get kicked off-campus. We had been lucky enough as it was that he'd been permitted to be around. Besides, two wrongs don't make a right.

"I love you two." I sighed. "What would I do without you?"

I fell asleep for the first time in a long time, feeling like I was right where I should be.

Chapter Five

I stood on the sidewalk, the skyline on the other side of the river lighting the night sky.

"Why do you keep doing this to yourself?" Reve appeared next to me and leaned on the railing. A railing that didn't protect someone's mother from throwing them over it and into the river below.

"I can't control it."

I turned towards the street, where a dark SUV sat idling at the curb. My father appeared with three goons surrounding him. Lilith's laugh filled the night sky.

I looked up, the sky dark with clouds. Lilith laughed again, this time from right next to me.

"Foolish girl. Did you really think everything was going to work out at the end of this?"

Just as my father reached forward, I was standing in the middle of a lush green field with mountains all around.

Reve gestured to a blanket and picnic basket laid out. "My lady."

I sat down, my mind now on what lay before me. For being a demon, Reve certainly was romantic. I guess he did have a lot of years of practice. How many women had he even been with?

"Where are we?" I opened the lid of the basket and pulled out a bottle of champagne. He took it from me and popped the cork.

"A figment of my imagination." He chuckled. "Also, a merging of different locations I've seen in movies."

"You have quite the imagination."

He pulled out two silver flutes from the basket and filled them. He could never go wrong with champagne. He pulled out a container of strawberries and melted chocolate. I wasn't sure how the chocolate remained melted, but it was a dream, of that much I was sure.

"I wish the others could be here with us." I took a sip of the crisp champagne and scrunched my nose as the bubbles fizzed in my mouth.

"They can be if you really want them to." It was the first time Reve had agreed to let me have them. I knew it wouldn't be the same as them in real life. "I'll have complete control of them." His grin grew as he watched my eyes widen. "Remember, you asked for it."

"Reve," I warned.

In the distance, three figures approached. I squinted my eyes because they were all the way across the field. As they got closer, a peal of laughter shot out of me. They were dressed in yodeler outfits, sans the shirts.

"I think it's a good look for them, don't you?"

I held my stomach as they got closer. They didn't speak

at first, but then Tobias opened his mouth, and a yodeling noise came out.

"Oh my God, make it stop." I fell back onto the blanket and covered my ears.

The yodeling stopped, and Asher, Tobias, and Olly disappeared. Reve appeared over me, grinning from ear to ear.

"You think you're so funny, don't you?" I lowered my arms from my ears to his chest. "You just have to have me all to yourself."

"I do. Can you really blame me?" He lowered his lips to mine. "If we could stay this way forever, I would."

I sighed and kissed him, wrapping my arms around him and pulling him closer. It would be so simple to stay in the dream world for eternity. Life would be easier.

I felt the pull of my consciousness and pulled away from him. I didn't want him to go.

He faded away.

WE FELL into a comfortable pattern of classes, training, and pretending the world wasn't about to face an unknown threat. Weeks passed, and Michael still didn't have a plan on how to get Lucifer back.

He was avoiding us. Well, mostly avoiding me. Every time he visited campus, he steered clear of my questioning gaze. No one else seemed to be as worried about the passage of time as much as I was.

I guess when you are practically immortal, a few

months feels like a few days. For me, it felt like years.

I walked into the gym for Weaponry class. It seemed like a waste of time since I would never be allowed to see any action, even if demons were pouring into the city.

Reve had shown us enough demon sketches that my mind was overwhelmed with what lurked on the other side of some invisible magical barrier. I wouldn't fight those things. Instead, I would do the smart thing and run.

My brain almost couldn't process it all.

I walked into weaponry class, wondering how the world was going to handle bug-eyed cat creatures that had nails as sharp as knives when Betty stepped into my path.

"Beatriz. Did you need something?" I crossed my arms and propped my hip to the side. It felt like the appropriate thing to do since I was in the angel version of some teen movie.

"Thanks to you, they are getting rid of divinity points." She spoke from her throat in the way only a bitch could.

"Oh. I'm sorry." I stuck my bottom lip out in a mock pout. "Did that make your self-worth go down?"

She smirked and examined her nails before looking at me again. "Just means that now we have nothing to lose."

"Is that a threat?" I stood my ground, even as she took a step closer. She smelled like she had on one too many squirts of perfume. I resisted the urge to gag. "Because that certainly sounded like a threat to me."

She shrugged and dropped her voice low. "I overheard a conversation about your mother."

My eyes widened, but I quickly schooled my expression. No one was supposed to know that Lilith was my mother. "About how she is Lilith, and how she has your father." She put her hand on my crossed arm. I looked down at it and then at her, narrowing my eyes. "Part of a guardian's duties is to protect from any and all threats. Michael doesn't seem to be doing his job anymore."

She patted my arm and stepped back, a smile on her face. Did she have some kind of God complex now? If these were the angels accepted into the academy, what were the angels who were rejected like?

"Are you sure you're an angel? I find it kind of hard to believe how you are even here. You have an ugly soul."

She laughed. "You aren't even an angel. I paid my dues."

"Is that how it works now? Blow jobs in exchange for wings?"

She was just about to step forward, probably to smack me, when Coach Ferguson blew his whistle.

She turned on her heel, and I followed to join the group of students already gathered around the coach. We had been practicing throwing knives at targets over the week. I managed to hit the target about half of the time. I wasn't the worst in the class, at least.

"Betty, why don't you demonstrate again for us how you angle your body to set up for the perfect throw." Coach Ferguson did not need to boost her ego any more than it already was.

Betty sashayed to the setup area. Of course, she had to be good at throwing knives. It seemed to fit her personality perfectly. She demonstrated by throwing two knives in quick succession at the targets. They hit the practice dummy right in the center of the chest.

"Perfect! Today I'm partnering everyone up! If you have mastered knife throwing, be prepared to help someone who hasn't." Great. Another opportunity to feel inferior to everyone else.

He started partnering us up. As the pairs split off, I stifled a groan. He paired up the two men that were left, leaving Betty and me.

"Betty, I trust that you understand the importance of getting Danica up to par with you."

He walked away, leaving me and public enemy number one to train together.

She made a face at the coach's back and then grabbed a set of knives. The knife-throwing dummies were set up around the perimeter of the gym so that no one would get nailed with a knife retrieving them from their dummy.

"Let's see what you've got." She handed me a knife and moved to the side. I threw the knife and barely hit the dummy's leg.

"It doesn't seem to help if I pretend it's you." I sighed and then smirked at her.

She snorted. "You have to pretend it's your worst enemy. I doubt I'm your worst enemy."

"Who's your worst enemy?" I watched as she balanced the blade on a finger. I had tried to do the same earlier in the week and damn near cut off a toe when I dropped it.

Lightning fast, she popped the blade in the air, caught it buy its hilt, and threw it at the dummy, hitting it right in the center of the forehead.

"My father." She walked to the dummy and pulled out the knives lodged in it.

I sometimes forgot that angels had once had lives that had led to their deaths. It was easy to forget when they were assholes to you. Case in point, Betty.

"Picture someone you despise more than anyone else in the world. Someone that hurt you so deeply that nothing can ever undo the pain." She handed me a knife. "You already have the proper form. Now you just need the right motivation to hit your target."

We practiced in silence until the coach blew his

whistle that time was up. I made my way to the dummy and yanked out the three knives lodged in its chest. Where the hell did the fourth go?

I felt a sharp sting on my cheek and then the clang of metal onto the gym floor. I reached for my cheek. The second I touched it, the sting of the slice caught up with me. It felt like a nasty paper cut from a thick piece of paper.

That fucking bitch cut me.

I charged at her before she even realized I was coming and tackled her to the ground. All of the training was paying off. I climbed on top of her and grabbed a fist full of hair. I brought my fist back to punch her. Before I could, a hand grabbed my arm and yanked me off.

"What the flying fuck is going on here?" Coach Ferguson yelled.

"Ask her! She threw a knife at me!" I gestured to my face that was dripping blood.

I never did understand how I could be half angel and half demon and still have no healing ability. One would think with the short end of the stick, there'd be some benefits.

He turned to glare down at Betty, who sat up and was rubbing her head like I had bashed it into the hardwood floor. I'd give her something to really rub her head about. I moved towards her again, and Coach Ferguson stopped me by putting out his arm.

"It was an accident." She made herself sound so

innocent. She looked up at the coach with tears in her eyes. "I tried to stop the throw, but she was already in its path. She must not have been counting the knives as we threw them."

I made one last move to attack her again, but he got in between us with his entire body.

"That's enough, Danica! Betty, apologize. Now." He should have sounded firm and angry that a student had been injured. Instead, he just seemed annoyed he had to deal with our brawl.

"That's it? Just an apology? She could have killed me! Or taken an eye out!" I could feel my face turning red as my anger bubbled up inside of me. "If this were any other school, she'd be expelled, or the police would be called. In fact, you know what! I'm pressing charges!"

Coach Ferguson put a hand on my shoulder. The move was meant to calm me down, possibly to get a grip on me in case I attacked, but all it did was piss me off more. I stepped back, shrugging off his hand.

"I'm sorry, Danica. Honestly, it was a mistake." She stood, and since the coach was focused on stopping me from wringing her neck, he didn't see her grin behind his back.

And to think, I had just been about to thank her for helping me.

~

I LOVED ASHER, I really did. But the second he found out about what happened with Betty, he decided that he would pair us up in a collaborative partnership during evening training.

As if forcing us to work together, would solve the more significant issue of her being a raging bitch. Rookie teacher mistake.

"When you're out there in battle, with bullets whizzing past your-" Asher was explaining the training we would be doing.

"We're going to have bullets flying at us?" Someone smarted off from the back of the group. A chorus of groans went up. Typically, that meant burpees for all.

Asher must have been in a good mood because he just rolled his eyes in response. "Hypothetically speaking. When you are being attacked, it's not going to matter who the person standing next to you is. You're a soldier. You're a unit. You are one."

I side-eyed Betty, who had a pout on her face. I was just as unhappy about being partnered with her as she was with me.

Asher rubbed his hands together like a mad scientist who thinks he has a good idea. Whether it was an evil gesture or an excited one was still up for debate.

"I've paired you up. Half of the pairs will be team A, and half will be team B." He held up touch-football mesh jerseys in two colors. "The objective is to make it to the other side of the field together as a pair. If your partner is knocked out, your job is to pick their ass up and carry them. Also, please remember not all of your classmates can heal."

After handing out the jerseys, we took our positions on the field. Those on team A were the "demons" and running through the field, and those on team B were angels trying to stop them.

This activity had disaster written all over it, especially for me.

"Maybe I should sit this one out," I said to Asher as he handed me and Betty blue jerseys. We would be pretending to be demons.

"You'll be fine. Betty should be taking the brunt of it." He nodded at Betty and then walked off.

I turned and looked at Betty, who had a smirk on her face. Great. Fantastic. I was going to end up in a wheelchair by the end of the activity.

We lined up on the edge of the field while team B spread out. When Asher blew the whistle, we took off at a jog. Other pairs seemed to be communicating, but Betty just headed straight through the center. I followed and kept up with her because I didn't have much choice. It reminded me of playing sharks and minnows in elementary school. Except instead of being frozen when you were caught, you were tackled.

We were doing great until a third-year, who

used to be a linebacker for his high school football team, barreled towards us. Betty was in position next to me to take the hit. He had even aimed himself at her.

Right as he was about to plow into her, Betty shoved me in front.

I fell to the ground with the behemoth of a man on top of me, and a sharp pain ripped through my knee. Why did men play tackle football? There was nothing fun about being hit by a wall of muscle.

"Shit, Danica! I'm sorry," Joseph said, scrambling up and holding out his hand.

I reached for it, and he pulled me to my feet. Pain radiated from my knee, and tears stung my eyes. I'd been injured more times in the past months living the life of an angel than in my entire existence.

"Fuck." I tried to put weight on my leg but almost fell.

Since my partner was already on the other side of the field, and I didn't want to risk getting hit again, I just plopped my ass down right in the center of the field and crossed my arms.

I saw red. Betty was a bitch. Asher was incompetent. Linebackers were way too strong for their own good.

"What the hell are you sitting in the middle of the field for?" Asher shouted from down the field. He was in the middle of the mayhem with angels tackling each other right and left. He clearly hadn't seen what happened.

Joseph jogged over to Asher and was speaking to him animatedly. Asher's eyes widened. He jogged over and squatted beside me. I glared nice and hard at him.

"Where does it hurt?" He touched my knee, and I hissed in pain. Tears were already streaming down my cheeks. They were a combination of anger and pain.

"Where does it hurt?" I couldn't believe him. "Don't touch me! I need to be healed. Since you aren't capable of that, get me someone who can." It was a harsh comment, but my knee was about to explode. I could see that it was twice the size it was supposed to be under the fabric of my capris.

He frowned and stood. He barked at Joseph to go get Olly, and then he stalked over to the other side of the field where Betty stood chatting with friends.

I could hear him yelling, but couldn't quite make out what he said. The end result was Betty bursting into tears, her wings extending, and her flying off towards her building.

Tobias, who had been on the sidelines reading his damn book again, made his way to me and scooped me in his arms.

"Maybe pay a little more attention instead of reading, Mr. Armstrong," I gritted out. "What's even the point of this bull shit? Are demons going to be tackling angels?"

"We don't know what's in store for us." Tobias set me down on a chair just as Olly jogged over to us.

"What happened?" He knelt in front of me, and then ripped the fabric of my capris up past my knee. I cried even more because they were my favorite Lululemon capris. "It's dislocated."

"Your fucking boyfriend wouldn't let me sit out." I winced as he put his hand over the knee. His hand glowed, and the pain receded instantly.

"Look at Tobias for me." He waited for me to look away, and then I heard a pop. "You're good to go. It might still feel a little tender."

Without waiting for a reply, he took off, jogging towards his section of the field. He seemed to be in his element with the teaching thing. I had even heard several students making comments on how he should become a teacher at the academy.

He did have the patience of a saint.

Tobias helped me stand and put his arm around my waist. "Let's get you back to the room. I think you need to rest that knee."

By the time we were back in the room, my knee felt perfectly fine. The walking seemed to have stretched out whatever remaining discomfort there was.

"Shouldn't you go supervise Asher?" I stripped my shirt off and threw it in the laundry basket.

"Are you going to be okay?" Tobias didn't just mean my knee.

"I'm fine *now*." I was only talking about my knee. I wouldn't be fine if we never made a move to rescue my dad. It seemed everything we were training for was to protect Earth, not save my father.

How could we just leave him with Lilith? There should be more urgency in finding him. His blood was powerful. *He* was powerful.

Tobias watched me as I took off the rest of my clothes. He cleared his throat as I walked into the bathroom.

"I'll see you later, then, after training." He turned and left, leaving me to fume.

Smart man.

"DANICA. CAN WE TALK?" Asher poked his head inside the room about two hours later. I had managed to take my mind off Betty but still found my mind drifting to thoughts of my dad.

I looked up from my studying and narrowed my eyes at him. Now I was reminded of my knee and the gash on my face. Both healed to perfection by Olly.

Asher slid into the room with Olly behind him.

"Where are Tobias and Reve?" I turned back to my notes.

"Where do you think? The game is on."

I grunted and tried to focus on my notes. I could feel both of them watching me. I imagined they were having a silent conversation behind my back with hand gestures and faces. I'd caught them once when I was in a particularly bad mood one day.

"Danica." Asher sighed.

I dropped my pen and swiveled in my chair to face him. "*What*?"

"I'm sorry."

I crossed my arms and stood. "You knew she had it out for me, and you deliberately paired us up. I told you I should have sat out."

He frowned and looked at Olly like he would fix the problem. Olly shrugged his shoulders.

"I thought-"

"Well, clearly, you thought wrong. What if he had broken my neck instead of dislocating my knee? What if Betty had shanked me in the kidney?"

I caught Olly smiling and leveled a glare at him. His smiled dropped.

"I'm serious. She is just the type to carry a shank on her. One second she'll be smiling and flipping that hair of hers, the next she'll be gutting me like a fish. Is that what you want? Fillet of Danica?"

He stepped towards me. "I said I was sorry. I thought it might help your dislike for each other if you had to work together towards a common goal."

I let him pull me towards him, and he wrapped his arms around me. He kissed my temple and then looked at me with a serious expression. "All right, how many orgasms is this going to take? At least three?"

"You can't just give me orgasms and expect me to-" His lips collided with mine, and I moaned.

Maybe my forgiveness could be bought with a kiss as good as the one he was giving me. His tongue probed, and I opened my lips for him. I really wanted to stay mad. When everything was falling apart, being angry felt right.

I was backing towards the bed when the door burst open, causing all three of us to nearly come out of our skin. For once, it wasn't just Asher on edge.

"A large group of demons has gotten through at Griffith Observatory. Let's go!" Tobias was frantic. "There are already civilian casualties."

"Shit!" Asher and Olly moved towards the door. I grabbed my shoes and sat down on the bed to put them on.

"You aren't going." Tobias shut the door because there was a lot of commotion in the hall as staff members grabbed their gear from their rooms.

"Why not? I could help!" I dropped my shoes and grabbed my boots instead. "I could stop them."

"Only staff are going. You'd just be a distraction."

The comment burned in my gut, and I crossed my arms over my chest.

"You aren't ready yet, Danica. We would be worried about your safety the entire time. Please don't take it personally. No students are coming this time." Tobias kissed my cheek, and then the three of them left without me.

Chapter Six

Asher

I felt like I was back at war again. Rushing around, grabbing gear, leaving the one I loved behind to protect others.

I thought I'd be fine since we didn't use guns or explosives. Demons didn't either.

That didn't stop the dread from welling up in my gut as we gathered in the parking lot of the academy. Other guardians from throughout the Los Angeles area were meeting us at the observatory, which as of five minutes ago, was being infiltrated by several dozen demons.

Demons that had somehow gotten through the barrier between Inferna and Earth. Lilith was making her move, and we were far from prepared. The academy students sorely lacked combat skills.

The angels in charge of coverups were going to

have quite the task keeping a hoard of demons attacking a tourist trap under wraps.

We landed on the side of the observatory and joined the other angels already gathered. A few looked in my direction and then narrowed their eyes. Word on the street was that I had been nick-named Snap.

"Thorne, are you going to be able to follow orders tonight?" one of the angels said, jabbing me in the shoulder with his finger. I resisted the urge to grab that finger and snap it in half.

"Fuck off, man. I said I was sorry for snapping your neck." I was still getting shit for snapping necks when we infiltrated the angel blood draining opera-tion. "Look at the bright side, it meant one less draining since you had to heal."

"I still wake up with a crick in my neck every morning."

Michael landed in the center of our group, and everyone fell silent. "We have at least three dozen demons we're dealing with. Several are inside. We'll first take care of the ones outside. There will most likely be casualties tonight, but if we have each other's backs, we won't see as many as they do." Michael looked around the group. "Now, let's go kill some demons!"

He took off around the side of the building and into a grassy area at the front. The others followed.

"Fuck, fuck, fuck." My feet seemed to be cemented to the ground. Everyone else was headed out there with swords raised, and I was frozen.

"Deep breaths." Toby appeared in front of me and put his hands on my shoulders.

Toby didn't realize it, but he did the exact same thing back in the war on multiple occasions.

I shut my eyes and took several deep breaths before opening them again. I was a little calmer, but the feeling of dread still coursed through my veins. I don't know why I thought I would be suited to fight.

"You good?" He stepped away and unsheathed his sword.

"I'm never good." I pulled out my own sword and met Olly's concerned eyes. "Don't you dare look at me like that. Take care of yourself, angel baby. The second you worry about me out there, we're both dead men. Well, angels."

I took off after Toby. I was fairly certain that Reve was nearby, but he was incognito. It was a minor comfort that the demon we had grown to trust had our backs.

The area at the front of the building was already pure chaos. Demons that looked human, but clearly weren't judging from their fangs and blood running down their chins, were dodging our swords faster than humanly possible.

Angels were fast, but they weren't vampire fast.

I shouldn't have been surprised there were vampire demons. After all, I was an angel. Still, seeing one up close and personal was a mind fuck.

I rammed my sword into the gut of a nasty looking demon that looked like a science experiment gone horribly wrong. It had the body of a wolf, the tail of a serpent, and the head of a raven. It fell to the ground, and I swung my sword to take off its head.

Danica had wanted to come along for this shit show, yet the woman couldn't even kill a spider without squealing. She'd lose it seeing some of these demons.

"Ugh, guys?" Olly shouted over the sounds of dying demons and swords slicing through flesh and bone.

I turned in his direction. It was just like in the movies. The moment some crazy-ass monster appears, and everyone pauses because, holy fuck.

It was at least ten feet tall and looked like one of the rhinos from *Ninja Turtles*. Angels and demons alike dove out of the way as it barreled straight towards the Astronomers Monument. It must have thought the six astronomers depicted on it were actually people because it began punching Galileo in the face.

While it was occupied, Ferguson and Michael tried to incapacitate it. It wheeled around and sent them flying. With a roar mightier than any lion, it took off, charging after Ferguson. It seemed to set its sight on him like a missile aimed at a moving target.

Several of us joined Michael in following as Ferguson ran into the observatory, trying to get away from the beast of a demon. The doorway didn't stop it, it just ran straight through the metal and bronze doorway.

It roared as a piece of metal stuck from its arm. It pulled it out and threw it, knocking over anyone and anything in its path.

It was like a bull in a china shop. Things that weren't even in the rhino demon's way were somehow broken and sent crashing to the ground. Ferguson was running around the Foucault Pendulum in the center of the room.

The rhino motherfucker had his sights set on goring him up the ass. Every time he'd get close, he would lower his single horn and surge forward.

It was only a matter of time before the rhino figured out it could jump across the giant circular hole housing the ball of the pendulum.

"I'm going to jump on it," Olly shouted over the noise and moved closer.

I wanted to tell him to use some common sense. Jumping on the back of a pissed-off demon was idiotic, but just as I opened my mouth, the side door burst open, and more demons poured in.

Was this it? Was this how I was going to die for the third time? It was doubtful I'd be given another chancc. Angels weren't like cats. We didn't get nine lives.

I took a few more demons out when I heard a man scream. Nothing was worse than hearing agony pour out of a fellow soldier's mouth. It was the antecedent of something really fucking bad.

I was on the far side of the room by the doors leading into the main planetarium. The irony of angels and demons fighting in a place that studied the sky was not lost on me.

The last demon near me went down with a thud, and I rushed forward towards the pendulum. What looked like gremlins were swarming over the sides and into the hole. More screams, this time frantic, erupted from inside of it. Someone was down there.

I backed up against the wall, my arms and legs not wanting to cooperate any longer. The sounds bombarded my ears until the only thing I could hear were the screams of agony. I slid down the wall to the ground and put my hands over my ears. I watched as Michael flew over the hole, trying to get into it and save whoever was down there.

My eyes darted around the room. I hadn't seen Toby or Reve since Galileo's head went flying and shattered into hundreds of plaster pieces. A panic set into my chest as I scanned the room for Olly. Headless demon bodies were scattered around, as well as a few downed angels.

"Stand back!" Michael's voice echoed through the rotunda. The hole the Foucault Pendulum was in lit up like a bonfire.

The shrieking of the gremlin-looking demons was deafening, and I covered my ears. I tried to get to my feet but was frozen with an unrelenting dread.

Demon heads and bodies were thrown in the fire.

"Asher? You doing all right?" Reve's voice came from next to me, and then he appeared. He looked fresh as a daisy.

"Olly," I managed to grit out. My mind was telling me to run away from this hell we had been thrown into, but my body wouldn't cooperate. I hadn't shut down like this since the day my lieutenant had his brains blown out right next to me during the liberation of a small town in Belgium.

"He's outside. The Behemoth took him for a little ride, but Olly killed it. You should have seen it! It was-"

A door burst open, and several vampires poured in. At least that's what they appeared to be.

Reve vanished and took one out from behind in a swift move that sent the head flying clear across the room. I hadn't seen Reve in action before, and it was something to behold. It was like the blades he was wielding were an extension of him as he sliced and diced the small cluster of vampires.

"Prince Reve?" A vampire stopped in its tracks, and its eyes went wide in recognition. He fell to his knees and lowered himself down in a submissive position in front of Reve.

What the actual fuck?

He hadn't told us outright that he was a prince,

we just assumed. Hearing it from a demon's mouth was just another cluster fuck to add to the ever-growing pile.

"We thought you were dead."

Reve needed to kill the fucker before he jumped up and ripped out his throat.

"Why are you here?" Reve still had his knives ready but had relaxed slightly. I looked between him and the vampire.

I managed to pull myself to my feet and put myself behind Reve. If he wasn't going to take out the vampire yet, I didn't want to be anywhere near it.

"She ordered us to." He looked up but avoided making eye contact with Reve. Instead, his eyes landed on me, and a chill ran up my spine.

"Why?"

Instead of answering, the vampire got a pained look on his face. He then dug into his chest with some kind of crazy hand strength and ripped out his heart. It was almost like he had been compelled to kill himself if captured. A cyanide pill would have done the trick. But then again, these were demons we were talking about.

I cringed as the body fell with a thud, and the heart, still beating, landed near Reve's boot.

"Fuck." Reve stabbed the heart, and blood pooled around it.

I was going to be sick.

I turned to find somewhere to vomit in peace.

The fighting was over. Angels were scattered around the room. Some grabbed the limp bodies of other angels and went out the doors with them.

The smell of burning flesh hit me in the face as I staggered past the fire. Michael gave me a concerned look as I passed by him but didn't stop me.

I managed to make it outside the doors before hurling the contents of my stomach into a bush. Besides my retching, there was silence.

I braced my hand on the side of the building and turned my head to look for the others. Reve had stayed inside with Michael, but I hadn't spotted Toby or Olly yet.

Stumbling down the stone steps, I stopped to put my hands on my knees. Maybe I wasn't cut out for this job anymore and should hang up my wings. Heaven was one of the best retirement communities.

A pair of boots came into my line of vision. They had splatters of blood on them.

"Asher." Olly's voice was like music to my ears.

He grabbed my arm and pulled me up to my full height. He looked like he had taken a ride on a massive demon. His cuts and bruises were healing before my eyes.

He cupped my cheek, and I felt the familiar warmth spread through my body. I didn't know how he fucking did it. He was a miracle worker, keeping me sane when I should very well have been rocking myself back and forth in a padded room.

"You're going to drain yourself," I warned, clasping his wrist and trying to pull his hand away.

He grunted and slid his thumb over my bottom lip. "I'll be fine."

"You shouldn't have done that. That was stupid." I took in the sight outside. It was like a war zone. Piles of demons were being prepared to be burned.

"Where's Toby?"

"Making sure humans don't see what's going on here. He's fine."

I breathed a sigh of relief.

A cleanup crew arrived, and I watched in fascination as they made quick work of cleaning up the evidence that anything crazy had happened. Galileo was a goner, but vandals were always destroying shit; it wouldn't be entirely out of the ordinary.

"Gather round," Michael bellowed from the top of the steps.

Everyone looked worse for wear, with several angels missing. I couldn't quite figure out who. Toby came to stand on the side of me that Olly wasn't on and put a hand on my shoulder.

"We lost five tonight. Moore, Reed, Sullivan, Nguyen, and Ferguson." He paused and looked up at the sky. "We're going to need to step up the training at the academy. The attacks are only going to get worse."

THE LAST PLACE I wanted to be was at the academy. I desperately needed to take the edge off. So, instead of heading back right away, we went to my building to shower and change. Reve went to his place, Tobias to Danica's, and Olly and me to mine.

What I really wanted to do at some point was knock a hole in the floor and build stairs. It wouldn't be too difficult of a remodel.

I texted Danica that we were safe. She was probably still pissed that she didn't get to join in on the action. She could be mad all she wanted. Our job was to keep her safe.

"Are you sure you're okay?" Olly asked as the door shut behind Reve and Tobias. Three bathrooms was the perfect number for our family of five. I was determined to make the three separate living spaces one mega space.

"I said I was fine." I went to my liquor cabinet and pulled out a new bottle of whiskey. I heard Olly sigh from behind me.

I was trying to cut back, but it was hard. Life just kept throwing curve balls my way. And now, with being on that damned academy campus all the time, I was struggling to maintain my calm persona.

I laughed as I thought about describing myself as calm. I poured the whiskey into a glass, and the smell filled my nostrils. Even the smell was a comfort.

I felt him move close behind me as I braced one of my hands on the counter. He slid his arm around me and worked my belt buckle loose.

"You don't need to drink." His mouth was on my neck before I could pull away, and I shifted my head to the side.

I let out a breath and then brought the glass to my lips and took a sip. "Tell me what I need then."

My belt was undone, and then he was unbuttoning my pants. His breath was hot against my neck as he worked the zipper down. We were supposed to be showering, not messing around.

An image of him taking me against the counter flashed through my mind, and I shuddered as my dick gave a happy little jerk and came to life.

"People died tonight, Oliver." I groaned as he worked my pants down past my ass and pressed against me.

I could feel his hard length and braced my other hand on the counter, forgetting my drink for the time being.

"I know." He rubbed against me. One of his hands went over the top of mine, and he reached the other around and grabbed my cock. "I need a reminder that you're still here."

I turned my head to the side, and he kissed the corner of my mouth. My dick slid through his fist as I rocked my hips.

"Get on the counter."

I loved when he got bossy with me. He saved

that side of himself for me, and it made my heart flutter. Yeah, he had me dick whipped. If there was such a thing.

I turned and jumped up. I kicked my boots off as he yanked his shirt over his head. My pants fell down my legs and gathered at my ankles. He slid his hands down to where the pants were stuck on my heels and took them off the rest of the way, along with my socks.

"Take off your shirt." I complied and sat bare on the cold counter with him looking at me with a hunger I hadn't seen in a while.

He took me in his mouth without any teasing and gripped me at the base. I groaned and buried my fingers in his hair. I had urged him to grow it out a little more so I would have more to hold onto, but he liked it short.

"Jesus, angel baby." I was nearly at the back of his throat and felt my balls tighten. He was sucking on me like it would be the last time he'd have a taste.

I leaned my head back against the shelf and willed myself to hold onto my load.

My dick popped out of his mouth, and he pulled me towards him as his wings spread. I may have squealed like a little girl as he flew us to the bed and dropped me in the center.

He removed his pants and settled between my legs.

"I want inside of you." His lips crashed into

mine, and he rubbed against me. I slid my hands to his ass and dug my nails in.

"Not ready for *that*." I groaned as he lowered his lips to my nipple and swirled his tongue around it. "Are *you* ready?"

"You just want to be first." He bit my nipple, and I smacked the side of his head. "Ow!"

"You know I have really sensitive nipples."

He smirked and leaned down and kissed it before his hand gripped us both. "If you can handle my fingers, you can handle my dick."

I was pretty sure his dick was substantially bigger than his damn fingers. I bucked my hips against him then rolled us so I was on top. "Let me fuck you, Oliver."

"Such a nice way of phrasing that. Let me roll right over." He rolled his eyes and groaned as I reached down and stroked him between his balls and his tight hole.

He sure had gotten mouthy. Danica liked to give me a hard time about how I was corrupting innocent little Olly, but I was convinced he was never that innocent to begin with.

"What would you prefer I say? Dearest Oliver. Let me make sweet man love to your ass?"

He chuckled and pinched my ass cheek. "Get the lube."

I reeled back and narrowed my eyes in suspicion. We always joked about going all the way but never ended up going through with it. It was a big step. It made me feel like such a virgin. Well, at least an ass virgin.

"You're serious?" I raised an eyebrow.

He cupped my cheek. "Either you're going to be inside me, or I'm going to be inside you."

"Fuck." I rolled off him and grabbed the lube from the bedside drawer. "Spread your legs."

He bit his lip and spread open for me. This was really fucking happening. My dick twitched in anticipation, and I damn near told it to calm the fuck down.

I worked my lubed finger inside of him and stroked his prostate. I could hardly wait until I could stroke it with my dick. I worked in a second finger and rolled him onto his side.

"Give it to me, Asher."

I was about to come from just his words.

I grabbed the bottle of lube and covered my dick in it before squirting some down his crack.

I scooted behind him and slowly eased in. He was so fucking tight, and I bit the inside of my cheek to stop myself from crying out. Once his ass hit my thighs, I stopped and reached around to grip his dick.

"Is it okay?" The urge to pound him into the mattress was strong.

"It's amazing." He pushed back against me, and I took that as my cue to start moving.

I tried to take it slow, but before I knew it, I had

him on his knees, my fingers digging into his hips to hold him in place.

He took over working his cock, his hand pumping faster than I had ever seen it move. We had waited too long for this.

The grunts coming out of his sweet little mouth sent me over the edge, and my balls tightened as my release slammed into me. Olly came with a grunt, and then we collapsed next to each other. I buried my face in between his shoulder blades.

Olly's shoulders started to shake, and my stomach dropped. "Did I hurt you?"

A laugh ripped out of him. "I landed in my own cum."

I groaned a laugh and sat up, looking down at him. "I love you. You know that, right?"

His laughter faded, and he pushed himself up to take my face in his hands. "I do." He kissed me gently. "I love you too."

We made our way into the bathroom. My chest felt tight, and for once, it wasn't because I was about to have a panic attack. It was because my heart was fuller than it had ever been.

Chapter Seven

Danica

I felt useless staying behind while everyone went to kick demon butt. Yes, I had just been angry about being included and then injured in a training exercise, but this was different. This was real. People's lives were at risk.

Wasn't I supposed to save the light from the dark? How could I do that if I was sitting on my ass at the academy? I should have been fighting. I could have possibly incapacitated a demon enough for a more capable angel to kill. Hell, maybe I could have even brought them all to their knees.

I scrolled through my phone, scouring the internet for any mention of demons or monsters attacking in the area. I even scanned the police logs.

There was nothing. It was probably for the best. People would lose their shit if they knew what existed on the other side of some magical barrier.

A magical barrier that could easily be manipulated with angel blood and opened completely with my father's blood. Supposedly.

If it was so simple, wouldn't Lilith have blown the barrier wide open by now?

I sent Ava a text. She was working, but usually, she called me on her breaks. Never in a million years did I think I'd be the one still in school, and she'd be the one with a full-time job.

The charges in her breaking and entering case had been dropped, but the damage was already done. Stanford hadn't rescinded her admissions, but Ava had decided to take a gap year.

My best friend, the one who had straight As and perfect attendance, had decided to have a quarter-life crisis.

I couldn't say I blamed her. I was on the verge of one myself. I needed a year off. Or maybe ten.

Fifteen minutes later, my phone rang with an incoming call from Ava.

"Girl, you will not believe the juicy piece of gossip floating around Blue Wave," Ava said as soon as the call connected.

"Hi to you too." I laughed.

Blue Wave was the hottest restaurant and bar in Santa Barbara. It was also the reason Ava was taking a break from school. She said it made her feel alive. I wasn't sure how swimming around in a tank all evening with men gawking at her seashell bikini top made her feel alive.

"I'd like to think we're past the stage of pleasantries." I heard a beep, and then the sounds of the restaurant disappeared. "So, do you want to hear what is making the rounds tonight at the bar?"

Gossip was just what I needed to distract myself from the fact that my guardians were somewhere fighting a hoard of demons without me.

"Sure, go for it." I sat in my chair and propped my feet on my desk.

"So get this, they found Dr. Adamson's body in some abandoned warehouse in Asia. He had a giant crescent or something carved on his chest."

I gripped the phone in my hand. "What?"

"He had been dead a few months. Isn't that crazy? I guess karma got ahold of him for all that weed he sold to high schoolers."

My heart was pounding so hard that I wondered if Ava could hear it on the other end of the phone. My feet slid off the desk, and I damn near fell out of the chair.

"Dani, you there?" She sounded concerned. I had gone radio silent.

"Yeah. It's just, that was it? They just found his body?" I stood and started pacing. Hadn't Lilith been using him to run her experiments on blood? Why would she kill him? Unless she had gotten what she wanted and didn't need him to experiment anymore.

"That's all the information anyone has. I feel a little bad for John. He was already pretty fucked up, and now with his dad being murdered..." She sighed.

While I understood her bleeding heart, I wouldn't go as far as to say I was sorry for John. I didn't know if that made me a horrible person or one that just saw things for what they really were.

I cleared my throat, still processing the fact that Lilith had killed John. Had she killed my father? Would she?

"I miss you. I can't believe your school wouldn't let you leave for the summer. See, this is why you should have taken a gap year too." I was grateful she changed the subject before I had more time to think about Lilith killing the doctor and leaving him to rot in an empty building.

"I feel like my entire life has been a big giant gap year." I sat back down in my desk chair and spun a few times. "I actually like my classes. Maybe I just needed to find something I was interested in. Math and studying poetry were definitely not my thing."

"Sir, you aren't supposed to be back here." Ava's voice was muffled like she was holding her phone against her shirt. "What are you-" Her scream pierced my eardrum, and I nearly dropped the phone.

"Ava?" I jumped out of my chair, sending it toppling onto its side.

There was scuffling, and a grunt before the line went dead.

With shaking fingers, I called her phone back. It went to voicemail. I tried calling again.

Damn it.

I quickly slid my feet into my shoes and took off out of my room like a bat out of hell. The building was empty since most of the staff were off fighting.

I ran as fast as my hybrid ass could to the first student building, which was where Cora and Ethan lived.

No one answered when I pounded on Ethan's door. I took the stairs to the next floor and banged on Cora's door. Where the fuck were they?

Panicking, I called their phones. Wings would come in handy right now.

I was pacing in front of Cora's door, trying them again and again when the elevator slid open, and Betty sauntered down the hall. You know, because my night wasn't shitty enough already.

"Eve. What an unpleasant surprise. Please tell me you aren't stalking me now." She looked me up and down with a scrunched-up nose.

"Have you seen Cora or Ethan?" I bit out. I was half tempted to call one of the guys but knew they wouldn't answer either.

"Do I look like your personal surveillance?" She rolled her eyes and stopped at her door with her keys in her hand.

"Goddamn it! Can't you for one second not be

such a bitch?" I shoved past her but didn't make it very far before she grabbed my arm. "Don't touch me."

"What's wrong?" She wasn't sarcastic or condescending for once. "You aren't normally so... neurotic."

"What isn't wrong? I don't need this right now. What I need is a pair of goddamned wings!" I flung open the door to the stairs and ran down to the bottom floor.

Once outside, I tried to calm myself down. Good decisions weren't made when I was panicking. I called Ava again, her phone going straight to voicemail instead of ringing.

Maybe I could just ask a random student to take me to Blue Wave. Not every angel hated my guts. I would say that most tolerated my presence now.

The door to the building opened, and Betty stepped out. "Where do you need to go?"

I spun around and narrowed my eyes. There was no way she was about to offer to take me somewhere without some kind of strings being attached or a prank involved.

She would probably drop me and laugh as I splattered.

"What's your angle?"

"I'll take you where you need to go to make up for the injuries I caused earlier." She shrugged her shoulders as if what was happening wasn't a big deal.

It was a big deal. Betty did a complete one-eighty out of nowhere.

To say I was shocked by her offer to take me to Blue Wave was an understatement. I only hesitated for a second before accepting her offer. Beggars can't be choosers.

She wrapped an arm around my waist, and we shot into the sky. I kept my eyes closed and prayed she wouldn't let me go.

We landed and I breathed a sigh of relief. I was lucky she hadn't taken me somewhere and left me to find my own way back.

I rushed inside the restaurant, which was packed. There was no way anyone inside would have heard Ava scream. It had only been ten minutes; maybe everything was fine.

I should have called the police or the manager, but in my panic, I had only had one thought: get to Ava.

"Table for two?" The hostess asked as I approached the hostess station.

I looked over my shoulder to find Betty right behind me. I told her when we landed that she could go. I hadn't expected her to stay. She was probably collecting information to use against me.

"Ava. I need to find her."

The woman raised her eyebrows and took a better assessment of me. I'm sure I looked like hell after the day I had.

"She's on her break. Do you want a table in the

bar area? Otherwise, we have about an hour wait for a table."

"She was outside, and she screamed. Please, where's a security guard or the manager or someone!" I gripped the edge of the counter, and Betty stepped next to me.

"We aren't allowed outside on our breaks. Especially not the mermaids."

Did this hostess not understand simple English?

I was about to lose my shit when Betty slammed her hand down on the counter. "Get the fucking manager."

My eyes widened, and I looked over at her. She looked back and shrugged as if she did this all the time.

The hostess backed up several steps and then pressed a button on the phone. Less than a minute passed when a burly man joined the hostess.

"What seems to be the problem?" He looked confused as he took us in. At first glance, we looked like college coeds out for dinner.

Before the hostess could even get a word in, I repeated what I had already said.

"Come with me." He turned and headed towards a set of stairs. I looked at Betty, and she nodded before we followed the man with the word 'Security' on the back of his blue tee-shirt.

Upstairs appeared to be the VIP section. The mermaid tank extended up into the area, with a platform where they could get in and out of it.

"Wait here." The security guard was a man of few words. He opened a door that led down a hall and disappeared.

"I've heard they are going to open one of these places in the Los Angeles area soon." Betty was attempting to make small talk while we waited. "I wonder how much a gig like this pays."

"Thirty an hour plus tips for the mermaids." I nearly jumped out of my skin at the voice behind me.

I turned, and the security guard was back with a man that looked like his suit cost more than my car. I knew a quality suit when I saw one. My heart ached at the thought of my father.

"My friend, Ava. She was on her break and-" I felt like I had been repeating myself for hours.

"She's fine." He looked between Betty and me. "She's in my office."

Betty gripped my arm, but I ignored her.

"I want to see her."

He nodded and then opened the door to the hall.

"Danica," Betty whispered. "He's Fallen."

I didn't care what he was, as long as my best friend was in one piece. His office door was open, and when Ava saw me, she jumped up as fast as her mermaid costume would allow and threw her arms around me.

"How'd you get here so fast? Danica, you're squeezing me a little too hard." Ava pulled away from the hug. She had been crying but didn't look like she was hurt.

"Doesn't matter. What happened?" I should have planned a better response to her question. Ava was smart. There was no way she would let go of the fact that it had been barely twenty minutes since we talked on the phone.

Santa Barbara was almost two hours away. Maybe she'd believe we took a helicopter?

She sighed and sat back down. She looked over at the man who had brought us in to see her as he sat down at his desk.

"A man attacked her." He folded his hands over his stomach and leaned back in his chair. "I took care of the situation."

I looked at Ava, and she bit her lip. There was more to this than they were saying.

"Where's the man?" Betty asked from behind me. I had almost forgotten she was there.

"He's locked in a room downstairs until he can be taken care of." I looked back at who I assumed was Ava's boss.

"You mean until the cops arrive?" I raised my eyebrows.

I examined the man in front of me. He was slender but had broad shoulders under his suit jacket. His hair was black. He looked dangerous in a low-key kind of way.

"We can't call the cops on this one."

Ava made a whimpering sound from her chair,

and I sat down next to her, taking her hand. She looked pale and was trembling.

"He... he... he had fangs." She gulped and gripped my hand. "It was *him*."

I stared at her, and then my eyes widened. "What do you mean it was him?"

"The man from your house," she whispered. "That one I thought I was in love with."

Fuck. I thought my dad had banished him back to hell. Had he been able to get through the barrier?

"What does she mean the man from your house?" Ava's boss narrowed his eyes at me. "Who are you?" He looked from me to Ava. He should have been able to tell we weren't human.

"Who are *you*?" I demanded.

His hands were folded on his desk, and he was leaning forward slightly. "Kai Matsui. I'm the owner." He shook his head. "Stop doing that."

"Stop doing what?" As soon as I finished asking the question, it occurred to me that I was commanding him to answer my question.

He didn't answer and instead got up from his chair. Betty shifted uncomfortably from her spot by the door.

"If a vampire is visiting your house and then tracking down a girl like Ava, I want to know why." He moved his suit jacket back a bit, and I saw he had on a holster with a gun and knife.

"You aren't supposed to be carrying weapons."

Betty stepped forward as if she was going to disarm him.

I'd give it to her. She had some balls.

Kai snorted. "And I'm pretty sure you shouldn't be here right now." He looked at me. "Your signature doesn't look the same as hers. Why?"

Ava was looking between us with confusion written all over her face. I was going to have to tell her something. There was no way she wouldn't remember every detail of the conversation we were having in front of her.

"She doesn't need to answer to you. Should I give Michael a call? I'm sure he'd love to hear about the heat you're packing." Betty surprised me again. Mere hours ago, she was trying to get me killed. What had Asher said to her?

"That won't be necessary. I was only curious. Would you like to see her attacker before we dispose of him?"

From the corner of my eye, I saw Ava's face pale even further. I was surprised she hadn't dwelled on how quickly I had gotten to Santa Barbara. Or maybe she hadn't completely processed it yet.

Trauma could really do a number on the brain.

We followed Kai downstairs and through the bar area to the kitchen. He took a set of keys out of his pocket and unlocked a door off of a hallway.

As soon as we entered the storage room, the hairs on my arms stood on end. The vampire was sitting against a far wall with chains wrapped around his ankles and wrists.

"Chains will hold him?" I looked to Kai, who had just locked us in with the vampire.

"They do if they are from Heaven." I raised my eyebrows and then looked at the vampire.

He was definitely the one from my house. As soon as he recognized me, he let out a laugh that almost made me piss myself.

"Danica Deville. And to think I once thought you were a prostitute." He shook his head. "How is your daddy doing? Oh, wait..."

I regretted that I hadn't made Betty stay behind with Ava upstairs. She certainly didn't need any more ammo to use against me.

"Why are you here? How are you here?" I stepped closer, and his eyes seemed to look right through me. "Answer me."

He met my eyes. "I'm sworn to Lilith. You shouldn't be able to control me." He laughed. "But apparently you can."

"Do you know where she has him?"

"You are all screwed." He blinked a few times. "She's in the castle. In Inferna. That's where she has him."

I shut my eyes for a moment, and when I reopened them, he had his head cocked to the side. "You can stop her." I narrowed my eyes at him. "She's using Lucifer's blood to put a hole in the barrier. It won't be long before Inferna comes to

Earth."

"What the hell is he talking about?" I ignored Kai's question.

"How is she doing it? I thought she was giving demons angel blood."

"She is. But our bodies fight it and eliminate it pretty quickly. When we have an injection, we have a minute to get through to Earth if we're strong enough. The same with his blood. Plus, a little dark magic." He shifted on the floor like he was trying to move his hands up, but the chains were wrapped too tightly around him. "I'm telling you too much."

"Why are you after Ava?"

He coughed, and a trickle of blood ran out of the side of his mouth. "Pure... so pure." He toppled over onto his side and looked to be in pain. "You have to kill her." When my eyes went wide, he shook his head. "Lilith. Kill her before..."

"Before what?"

He passed out before he could answer.

Kai cleared his throat. "Is he serious?"

I looked down at the vampire and then turned towards the door. Shit was getting way too strange. It wasn't like I hadn't heard Michael or Reve talk about vampires, but seeing one was something else entirely. They looked human, well besides their pointy teeth. But the one laying on the ground didn't even have those out.

We had been learning about all kinds of

demons in Reve's training. Many of the myths humans believed in were a reality to some extent.

At some point, I needed to tell Ava about me. Her life had changed because of me. I at least owed her the truth. Maybe just after I saved the world from my mother.

I hesitated at the door and then turned back to face Kai. "Tell Ava I had to go. You'll make sure she gets home all right?"

He nodded, and Betty and I left Blue Wave.

WE LANDED outside the faculty building some-time well after midnight. The vampire wasn't dead but was close enough to death that there was no use in waiting around to see if he'd wake up again.

Betty started walking towards her building after we landed. I was still surprised she hadn't ditched me at Blue Wave.

"Betty." She turned back. "Thanks for helping me."

She sighed and took a step back in my direction. "Lilith is your mom, isn't she?"

She was smart, I'd give her that. I probably wouldn't have been able to connect the dots if it was me in her position.

I didn't answer.

"I wish I would have had the strength to kill my

father before he killed me." She swallowed hard. "Don't let us down."

I made my way into the building, mulling over her words. I wasn't a killer. Even if my mother needed to die, the thought of having to end her life made me feel sick to my stomach.

The faculty building was eerily quiet. Everyone should have been back by now. I ran up the stairs and down the hall to my room.

The room was dark, but I could make out forms lying on the floor. I turned on my cell phone screen for light and smiled, seeing they had pushed furniture against the walls and dragged the mattress to the floor. It looked like a second mattress was right next to mine.

I took off my clothes, leaving only my panties on, and slid in the middle. Arms wrapped around me.

"Where were you?" Reve's voice came from the end of the mattresses, and I felt the mattress dip by my feet.

I rolled onto my back, and he moved one of my legs so he could settle between them. He rested his head on my stomach.

"Ava needed help. A vampire attacked her."

"Vampire?" Asher mumbled next to me. He grabbed my hand. "How'd you get there?"

"Betty. What'd you say to her?"

"I told her to stop being a fucking bitch because you were about to save the world." He kissed my shoulder and snuggled closer to me. "I may have said a few other things that don't need repeating."

"How did everything go?"

I felt Tobias's beard against my other shoulder as he moved in closer. He and Olly had been quiet so far. Olly sounded like he was sleeping.

"We lost five. Ferguson and Nguyen are gone." Tobias's voice was sad, and I felt a tear hit my shoulder.

"Coach Ferguson?" There was no other Ferguson that I knew of. Sadness washed over me. Sure he hadn't been the nicest in the world to me, but over the past several weeks, he had been indifferent towards me.

I felt Tobias nod. I slid my hand into his and gave it a squeeze. I didn't quite know what to say to ease his grief, so I just laid there quietly, letting him rub his beard against my skin and squeeze my hand.

Sometimes just being there for someone was enough.

Chapter Eight

*W*hen an angel dies, their body is taken back to Heaven so their soul can be saved. No one was quite clear on the details when I had asked. Did the souls just float around like Asher's had? Did they get a second chance at being an angel?

There was a memorial on the football field the next night. The entire school plus several angels from outside the school showed up to light candles and tell stories about the angels that died.

I stood at the back of the crowd with Reve, both of us feeling out of place among the angels. He held my hand as we looked on.

Since I had woken up that morning, a feeling of dread had encompassed my every move. One of the dead angels could have been one of my angels. Every time there was a demon attack, the risk of losing one of them increased.

I couldn't handle the thought of one of them dying.

Asher's death had shaken me to my core. I couldn't go through that again.

After the service, we decided to take a case of beer to one of our favorite spots on campus. On the other side of the parking lot was a copse of trees that had a small clearing in the middle. Over the summer, we had set up Adirondack chairs and a fire-pit.

Tobias started up the fire while I passed beers around. I downed half the bottle before the others had even opened theirs.

"Whoa there, fish lips." Asher chuckled, popping the cap off of his. He took a long pull from it before setting it on the arm of his chair. "You've been quiet all day."

"Just have a lot on my mind." I finished the bottle and burped. A small price to pay for drinking it so fast.

I felt my cheeks flush with heat as the fire sprang to life in front of me, and the beer hit my blood. I reached forward and grabbed another bottle.

"Tell me about it." He watched as I took a much more reasonable swig.

"Did you know that John Adamson's body was found in an abandoned warehouse?" I tapped my finger on the side of the bottle and then started to pick at the label.

Olly sat down on the arm of Asher's chair.

Asher looked up at him and then back at me. "We heard about it."

"You didn't tell me." A long strip of the beer label came off. I rolled it into a ball and then threw it into the fire. "What else haven't you told me?"

"There was no point in telling you." Tobias grabbed my hand and yanked me up before sitting in my seat. He pulled me into his lap.

I protested with a grunt, but he had already secured an arm around my waist.

"What happened to no secrets?" I frowned at him as he grabbed my beer and took a drink. "That's mine."

I snatched it from him. John dying seemed like a mighty big secret to keep from me. What else weren't they telling me?

"You're stressed enough as it is." Reve joined us and grabbed a beer. "Your nightmares are just now starting to lessen. We felt it was in your best interest to keep it to ourselves."

"My whole life is a nightmare, Reve." I leaned back against Tobias. I was still mad, but not enough to deny myself the comfort he brought me. "What else?"

They hadn't answered it the first time I asked. Maybe they thought I would forget..

They all went silent, the only sounds the crackling of the fire and the chirps of crickets.

"Tobias?"

He sighed. "Michael is planning a mission to Inferna. He wants us to go. You included."

"I can't go to hell. My body can't handle it." The thought had already crossed my mind. How were we supposed to save my father if he was there and we were here?

"Rafael thinks that was because you went before you had matured. He thinks you could handle it now." He cleared his throat. "He also already took a blood sample there to see how it would react."

I made a disapproving sound in my throat. Everyone was always fucking with my blood. I was one big walking, talking science experiment.

"Then what are we waiting for?" I looked amongst them. "If we don't stop her, we're all going to die."

"That's an overly dramatic way of looking at it." Asher finished his beer, and Olly grabbed him another. We all needed the booze after the last two days we'd had.

I looked down at my beer bottle. "What if one of you dies trying to protect me?"

Tobias put his chin on my shoulder. "We know what we signed up for. As guardian angels, it's our job to protect and defend from the darkness."

"And my job as a has-been prince is to keep my people at peace." We all looked over at him. It was the first time he had referred to himself as a prince. "Plus, to protect you."

"I don't know if I can live with myself if one of

you..." I choked on my words and squeezed my eyes shut.

"Dani. Our job is to make sure you're safe. We know what might be in store for us. If we weren't willing to make that sacrifice, we wouldn't be here with you." Asher reached across the gap in the chairs and took my free hand.

A tear slid down my cheek, and I wiped it away. No one spoke again for several minutes.

"I let Asher stick it in my ass," Olly said nonchalantly.

My eyes popped open and went wide. Reve choked on his beer and spit it out onto the dirt. A laugh bubbled out of me. It shouldn't have been funny, but Olly's delivery was perfect timing. For a moment, I forgot what I was so sad about.

"Jesus Christ. That was information I didn't need to know." Tobias's chest shook against me as he laughed. "Not that I think there's anything wrong with it."

"You should try it." Olly grinned as Tobias shook his head vigorously. "Come on. I'm sure Reve is willing."

"Reve is not willing." Reve stood and dumped the rest of his beer in the fire. He wasn't that big of a drinker. He looked at Tobias. "Want to finish up your tattoo tonight, since we might be going to hell soon?"

Tobias moved me off his lap. "Let's do it."

"Danica, want a tattoo? I brought all my stuff."

Reve looked down at me from next to the fire. The flames behind him made him look scary as fuck, and my heart sped up a little. He looked like he was going to eat me alive.

I scrunched my nose. I had no desire to get stabbed repeatedly by a needle. I didn't know how Tobias could tolerate the pain of repeated tattooing sessions.

We stayed outside a little longer and then went back to my room. It was a tight squeeze having two mattresses on the floor, but with tomorrow being a big fat question mark, we all wanted to be near each other.

I really couldn't explain the desire to be close. It was what it was. Now, it felt even more vital.

Reve set up his tattoo equipment and ink on the kitchen table, and Tobias sat in a chair. He already had most of his tattoo redone, but still needed to have Margie's face tattooed. The process required Reve to go over the same spot several times.

Olly hooked up his gaming system, and he and Asher started playing some game involving zombies. I was just glad they hadn't put on Fortnite.

"Do you think with everything going on, they're going to lessen our workload?" I pulled one of my notebooks out that was filled with notes. I had to review what I wrote after classes because I tended to mindlessly take notes.

"Probably." Tobias took his shirt off and nodded to the chair opposite him. I moved from my desk to the table with my notebook. "Not that I would know."

"I'm sorry." Guilt twisted in my stomach. I felt partly to blame for his suspension. If it had been any other student, Sue Whittaker wouldn't have come down so harshly on him.

"You don't need to apologize." Tobias winced as Reve started working on his tattoo. "Maybe it's time for a change."

"You can come work for me." Asher somehow managed to pay attention to our conversation and stab a zombie without looking away from the screen.

Tobias grunted and shook his head. "I was thinking of writing a book."

I opened my notebook and looked down at my chicken-scratch handwriting. Half the battle was reading my notes. The teachers talked so fast I had to sacrifice legibility for something that looked like a doctor wrote it.

"A book would take you like what? A week?" I started underlining and circling parts of my notes with a Flair pen. I'd rewrite what was most important.

"I think a book takes a little longer than that to write. What would you write a book about?" Reve didn't take his eyes from the face he was drawing onto Tobias's skin.

"Love. Loss. Friendship. I don't know. It was just

an idea. It's not like I'm doing anything else at the moment."

I looked up, and Tobias was watching me. I smiled and put down my pen. "You could be my professional tutor."

"Tutors are paid good money. When I was a kid, my parents paid for tutors since going to school was out of the question." Reve put his tattoo gun down and swapped out the ink.

"There are schools in hell?" I wanted to know so much more about it but had never felt it was the right time to bring it up. "Like here?"

"Similar to here for the most part. Most demons live in villages with demons similar to them. Some don't go to school at all. The more human-like the demon, the more human things they do." Reve started to work again, never glancing up. "It's a little crazy how similar Inferna is to Earth. Well, at least for some things."

"Were you really a prince?" Leave it to Asher to ask the uncomfortable question. We had all been wondering if he was just yanking our chains.

"Yes. I suppose now, I am the king. Not that I would even want that job if I had the chance. I never wanted to be a king." He went back to tattooing.

"What about your siblings?"

"Even if they were willing, the first-born male heir to the throne always develops the gift of visions and a phantom form. The females have no special abilities, not even to produce nightmares. Dream demons have exclusively been the sole demon race on the throne because we can control others to an extent. Having a phantom form also prevents assassinations." He cleared his throat. "That is until Lilith."

Reve finished Tobias's tattoo and wrapped his arm in plastic wrap. The portrait of his family looked even better than it had before.

"Thanks, man. Maybe I will stop giving you so much shit about the Giants and Raiders."

"No problem. I definitely won't stop giving you shit over your teams." Reve put his gear away.

My phone rang, and I flipped it over to see who was calling. Why on earth would Michael be calling me? He never called me, opting to go through Tobias.

"It's Michael." I accepted the call. "Hello?"

"Danica." His voice was serious, not that he had any other tone. "I have some news about your father."

I gripped the table with my free hand and tried not to let the pounding of my heart consume me. Michael was quiet on the other end, waiting for me to respond. "Tell me."

"I was able to have a talk with that demon at Blue Wave. He told me much of the same information he told you." I wished he would get to the point. "Lilith is using the Holy Grail to perform a ritual with your father's blood and weaken the barrier."

"What are we going to do? How long can he...." Live. I didn't let myself speak it out loud. He could live forever, couldn't he? But what if one time she took too much?

"We leave tomorrow at sunrise."

"We?" The others gathered around the table.

"You five. I'll take you there, but then you'll have to go find him. We can't risk Lilith capturing any other original archangels or a large group of angels."

That left me with even more questions, but I was starting to realize that sometimes I didn't need an explanation for every single little thing. Some things were better left without an answer.

I let the phone drop to the table after ending the call and looked up. "I'm going to hell to look for my dad. I'll understand if you don't want to-"

"We're in this together." Tobias took my hand and then pulled me to him. "Stop questioning our devotion to you. We're all still here, aren't we?"

I bit my lip and searched his eyes. It's not that I was insecure, but I still had a hard time believing I had four men in my corner.

"We'll find him." Reve moved behind me and brushed my hair over my shoulder. "Even if it's the last thing we do."

I shut my eyes as he kissed the back of my neck.

It's like they knew when I was about to freak out and how to distract me from my thoughts.

"Let's take your mind off things for a bit." Tobias leaned forward and brushed his lips over mine. "I know exactly what will help us have a good night's sleep tonight."

My lips parted as Reve's hands slid around to the clasp on my jeans. Tobias's beard scraped along my jaw, and his lips brushed against my ear. My knees felt like they were about to give out on me.

I moaned as Reve popped the button on my jeans and pulled down the zipper. His hand slid into my jeans and found my clit through my panties. I whimpered.

I opened my eyes just in time to see Olly grab Asher by the belt loops and pull him towards him. He looked over at me and winked.

So this was actually going to happen. The night before we might all die. We were going to finally all have sex. Together. At least I thought that's what was about to happen.

I'd be lying if I said I hadn't done an internet search for how to be with four men at once. The results had left me wishing I would have brought my box of Barbies. You know, to see if it was actually possible.

Tobias grabbed my chin and brought my gaze back to his. He looked at my lips, and then kissed me. It was a kiss that told me to stop overthinking things and let myself go.

Reve was working my pants and panties down my legs while Tobias lifted my shirt over my head and unclasped my bra. I stood before them, baring everything. Four sets of eyes took me in. I shivered with desire, and my nipples tightened.

"Get on the bed." Tobias's voice had dropped a considerable amount. It was the lowest I'd heard it, laced with desire.

I crawled onto the mattress and laid on my back, sitting up slightly on my forearms. "Are you just going to stand there and stare at me or are you going to take your clothes off?" I looked at each of them, and they looked at each other.

I bit my lip and moved my hand down my body and spread my legs. Something about being naked in front of them all made me feel empowered. Like I could take on the world.

"I mean, you don't have to." I slid my hand between my legs. "I think I have my vibrator somewhere."

Clothes went flying, and I laughed at their haste. I wasn't sure what was about to happen, but the wetness and heat between my legs told me it could only work out favorably for me.

Asher was the first to make it to me and kissed me hard before moving his mouth to a nipple. He swirled his tongue around the tight bud and moaned as Olly moved behind him to kiss his shoulders.

I shut my eyes and turned off my brain. I

arched into Asher as Olly leaned over him to kiss me. A pair of lips trailed up my leg until they reached the apex and flicked my clit. I wasn't going to last long with four of them touching me at once.

I opened my eyes as the bed dipped, and Tobias laid on the other side of me. He stroked my hair and then ran the back of his hand up and down my side. Goosebumps spread across my skin, and he smirked.

"Want to know something funny?" Tobias's finger drew circles around the nipple that Asher wasn't flicking with his tongue.

I moaned, and my mouth opened in a pant. I didn't think it was the time or place to be talking but nodded my head anyway. It was hard to stay focused on any of them when Reve was swirling his tongue in the most sinful way.

"Olly went to Ikea and bought those little wooden artist dolls. He glued our faces on them and has been showing us different positions."

My laugh morphed into a moan. I moved my hips up to meet Reve's tongue as the pressure continued to build. I heard a bottle open, and then Asher moaned against my skin. Whatever Olly was doing behind him, he was enjoying, if his erection working against my leg was any indication.

Two fingers slid into my pussy as Tobias kissed me. He silenced my cry as my orgasm ripped through my body. Tobias rolled me on top of him and slid into me in one swift movement that made my core clench.

Reve moved to the front of me and stood over Tobias's head. "I hope you enjoy the view down there." He chuckled and moved forward for me to take him in my mouth. His hands went to my hair.

I was so blissed out that my mind wasn't even on the other two. It was hard keeping track of where everyone was when I could barely keep my eyes from closing.

Wet fingers slid between my cheeks, and I slid my mouth off Reve and looked back over my shoulder. Asher had his eyes on my ass as he slid a finger between the cheeks.

I groaned as he probed the tight hole and then slowly worked his finger inside. Olly was behind him doing the same. I raised an eyebrow.

"Don't even say anything, Dani." He shut his eyes for a moment then opened them. "I can't believe I'm about to lose my ass virginity."

I stifled a laugh and turned back to Reve, who was slowly stroking his dick. Asher slid into me, and Tobias grunted a curse under me. I took Reve in my mouth and flicked my tongue over the head.

It took a few minutes to find a rhythm, but soon the sounds that filled the room sent another orgasm crashing through my body. I dug my nails into Reve's ass cheeks, and he thrust deeper into my mouth, nearly hitting the back of my throat.

Asher's thrusts behind me got more erratic, and

he bit into my shoulder. I felt like I might float away as my entire body tightened again.

"Fuck," Reve grunted as he came. I swallowed all of him as another orgasm rocketed through me. That seemed to set off a flurry of cursing and grunts as a chain reaction of orgasms rolled through everyone.

Reve moved, and I collapsed forward on Tobias.

"I love you guys." I gasped. Tobias's chest shook as he laughed. "Don't laugh at me."

They could laugh at me all they wanted if they kept giving me orgasms. I just hoped it wasn't the last time I got to experience all of them at once.

After cleaning up, we fell asleep ready for whatever hell was going to throw at us.

Chapter Nine

$\mathcal{W}$e were supposed to leave at sunrise, but instead, we were jolted awake as the earth shook. I dove under the table like the well-trained Californian I was. Earthquakes and California went hand in hand. Earthquake drills were the norm in school.

The guys joined me under the table, with Olly looking the most disturbed by what was happening. When we were in Shanghai, the hospital had shaken slightly as the massive demon serpent flew towards it, but this was ten times worse.

This earthquake was much different than what I had experienced before. I wondered if the building was going to collapse. It lasted twice as long as a typical earthquake.

As soon as the shaking stopped, we climbed out from under the table and threw on our clothes. None of us spoke, because what do you say to each other when it's pretty apparent something substantial just happened?

Nothing.

You say nothing.

"It's demons." Reve appeared just before our phones started pinging with messages. He was out of breath and bent over with his hands on his knees.

I had gotten so used to him being invisible that I hadn't even realized he was missing when the earthquake started.

I grabbed my phone off the charger and swiped open the messages. Tobias came to look over my shoulder and then snatched the phone from me.

"Seriously?" I glared at him and tried to take the phone back.

"It's an emergency message from Michael." As if that gave him an excuse to be grabby with my phone. He pushed a few buttons. "A mass amount of demons came through at the same time."

"Through the ground?"

"The ground just happened to get in the way." Reve had finally caught his breath and was pacing while we finished putting on clothes and shoes.

I snatched my phone from Tobias's fingers and looked at the messages. It was a mass push message.

Over a hundred demons have broken through on the Griffith Observatory's grounds. More arrive every few minutes. All capable angels, including academy students, are requested immediately. Weapons will be available upon arrival.

My heart felt like it was coming up through my

throat. Had a hole been ripped through the barrier? Was hell about to come to Earth? Were we all going to die?

I tugged on my boots and jumped up once they were on. Four sets of eyes were watching me, then they looked at each other. I knew what they were thinking, and I wasn't about to let them leave without me.

"I'm *not* staying behind this time. What if I can control them? Isn't this the perfect opportunity for me to see what I'm capable of?" I crossed my arms over my chest.

Olly ran his hands over his head. It was a nervous movement I hadn't seen him do before. He looked at the guys again before stepping towards me and taking my hands in his.

"We don't want to-"

I pulled my hands away and backed up a step. "Don't give me that shit. I want to fight."

"You aren't ready, Dani." He made a move to grab my hands again, and I put them in my pockets. "We decided to keep you out of this for as long as possible."

I narrowed my eyes and saw Asher shift from one foot to the other. His unease was definitely warranted in this case. I was tired of being stuck on the fine line between fragile and badass. It was time for me to spread my hypothetical wings and fly.

"Let's just go. She'll get over it," Reve said.

Oh no, he didn't.

"I'm a grown-ass woman. Reve, you will take me." I cringed as I said the words, and saw the hurt on his face but then threw his words back at him. "You'll get over it."

Tobias cleared his throat from where he was watching the exchange between us. "Let's go. Reve. Go ahead and take her like she's requested. I'm sure your bike will get you two there in no time."

Shit, shit, shit.

My jaw dropped a bit as Asher, Tobias, and Olly walked past me and planted kisses on my cheek. They walked quickly out the door, leaving Reve and me in the room.

"What just happened?" I looked at the closed door and then to Reve, who had an amused look on his face.

"I certainly will take you." He pulled his keys out of his pocket. "We should get going, it will take us almost an hour to get there."

I followed him downstairs and out of the building, where angels were taking off in groups. Reve couldn't fly with me. It had been an oversight on my part. A foolish one.

Reve walked in front of me as we made our way to the parking lot. There was no way in hell I was going to sit for almost an hour on his crotch rocket. We were supposed to stick together. Save the light from the dark and all that bull shit.

How could we if I wasn't even included?

Before I could question my sanity, and before

Reve realized the wheels in my mind were spinning, I turned and ran towards the student dorm buildings.

Someone would take me. Even if I had to beg and offer them my first-born child or my car, I'd get someone to fly me to hell on Earth.

I heard Reve shout my name, but I was already closing in on the large clusters of students readying to take off from between the dorm buildings.

Spotting Ethan and Cora, I plowed through a few groups and nearly ran straight into them in my haste.

"Let's go now!" I looked over my shoulder and saw all the students I had just moved through part like the Red Sea for Reve.

Ethan's eyes widened, and he looked at Cora for direction. See, that's what the men were supposed to do; look to the woman for direction.

"You heard the lady! Let's go." Cora's wings snapped out with Ethan's following quickly behind.

Ethan grabbed me around the waist, and we shot into the sky. I was getting used to flying, finally, but still couldn't keep my eyes open. I'd rather not see how far my potential death lay.

We landed in a large parking lot. It was chaos as angels dashed around in search of weapons, which were piled on the asphalt. I managed to find a sword that was lightweight, and we ran towards the mayhem.

The noise level intensified as we got closer to the

actual observatory, or what was left of it. I had only seen it once on a field trip and remembered how amazing the building was.

Now, it was starting to look like a pile of rubble.

Angels were carrying other angels back towards the parking lot, while others flew past us right into the melee. My ears were ringing as screams and shrieks pierced them.

Several fires were spread out on the lawn, bonfire style. The smell made bile rise in my throat.

"Holy shit." Cora seemed to be frozen in place as her mind processed the scene before her.

I wanted to be frozen too, but a demon that looked like a science experiment gone wrong was headed straight for us.

Practicing with each other and on practice dummies was nothing compared to having a horse-sized demon that had the head of some kind of bird and the body of a dog, come barreling towards you. I certainly wasn't going to stay standing in its way. I grabbed Cora's arm and pulled her with me out of its path.

It was headed towards the parking lot, but just before it reached where the grass and cement met, two knives landed in its throat, sending it falling onto its side. Betty landed next to it and stabbed it in its heart before another angel came along to take its head.

She retrieved her bloody knives and then shot

back into the sky. I still didn't like her much, but that was a badass move she had just pulled.

"Where'd Ethan go?" Cora looked around frantically as we stayed glued to each other's sides.

We were out of our element. Coming here was a stupid idea. The amount of capability we had in us was about the size of our pinkies. At least that was the case when things were so crazy all around us.

Had there just been one demon, we would have been fine.

There were hundreds.

I needed to find my angels. I might not have known what the hell I was doing, but they'd help guide me. Or at least have my back.

A gremlin-looking creature seemed to come out of nowhere and attached itself to my boot. Thank fuck for knee-high boots because the little bugger couldn't bite through the leather, despite his best efforts.

Cora kicked him off and then brought her sword down on him, slicing him in two. Green goop coated her sword, and it suddenly smelled like cotton candy.

I couldn't resist the urge to take in the sweet scent and breathed in deeply. The world suddenly became much more vibrant and seemed to streak with rainbow colors. I looked over at Cora, who had dropped her sword and was examining her hand in fascination.

She had such gorgeous hair. It looked like a unicorn had painted it with all the colors of the rainbow. I dropped my sword and reached out my hand to pet it. It was so soft, like the fur of a chinchilla.

How did I even know what the fur of a chinchilla felt like?

"You're so pretty, Cora."

She touched my hair and nodded, her eyes glazed over and shiny in the light coming from the moon and fires. "No. You're the pretty one, Danica. You have four boyfriends. Four!" She burst into giggles, and so did I.

We wrapped our arms around each other in a hug.

"Fuck! You spilled its blood!" There Ethan was. Cora's face lit up like a Christmas tree. Really, like an actual Christmas tree.

Ethan rushed over to us and picked up my sword. He grabbed us and tried to pull us away from the cotton candy scent that made everything so lovely.

"No, Big E." Cora twisted out of his grasp and linked her arm with mine. "It's so perfectly lovely right here. Dani, I think you should leave your four boyfriends, and we can go get married."

I giggled, and both of us burst into laughter again. In the back of my mind, I knew that this wasn't the time or place to laugh like two cackling hyenas. I felt so free. So alive.

"You killed a Dulcis Fiend!" Cora cocked her head as Ethan chastised us. I didn't know what the hell he was talking about. "Oh my God, we need to move now!"

I didn't know what all the fuss was over. I was perfectly content where I was. We struggled with Ethan as he attempted to push us away from the really gross-looking animal on the ground. Where had that come from?

"Dulcis Fiends?" Cora shook her head and rubbed her eyes. "I killed... oh! Oh, my God!"

I glanced where her eyes were glued. I didn't see what the big deal was. They were kind of cute. There were about ten headed straight towards us.

Cora picked up her sword and pushed me behind her. "Damn it. Is this all of them?"

"How much did she inhale?" Just as the question left Ethan's lips, the demons made it to us and spread in a semi-circle.

Cora had a tight grip on my arm because I tried to walk forward to pet one. They looked like little old green grandpas. They were adorable.

"We have to burn them!" Ethan shouted as the sounds around us escalated. "Fuck!"

One of the demons was on Ethan's leg. He started shaking his leg to get it off. Just when it went flying, another one lunged for him.

"What's happening?" My mind was foggy, and I looked around. "What in the fresh hell are these things?"

I grabbed my sword out of Ethan's hand.

"Don't kill them with a sword!" Cora was attempting to get two off Ethan's leg.

"Hey!" I shouted. "Get off him!"

Ten sets of beady little eyes turned to look at me. My eyes went wide, and I backed up a step. This was like the scene out of Jurassic Park when the Dilophosaurus stares at the nerdy guy right before it kills his ass.

"Send them home," Reve said from next to me.

"Go home!" They hesitated for only a moment before they ran towards the observatory.

"Fuck, my leg." Ethan was now on the ground holding his leg. "It's not healing. Why isn't it healing?"

He was panicking. Two angels jogged over to us and picked him up. Cora looked torn between going with him and staying with me. Hell, I wanted to go with her.

"Go, I'll be fine."

Would I be fine? Would Ethan be fine?

She gave my arm a squeeze and then ran after the angels and Ethan towards the parking lot.

"Let's go." I looked in the direction of Reve's voice. He was pissed. "Now."

"But I can help! You saw me! I can send them home!" I turned back towards the observatory.

"Danica." His hand wrapped around my arm. "You think you're helping? You just signed Ethan's death certificate. Now, let's go before-"

"What do you mean I signed his death certificate?" I turned to where I knew he was. His hand was still on my arm.

"Dulcis Fiends have venom that is so potent that one drop of it can kill two thousand people."

"He'll be fine. The healers will take care of it." Reve didn't reply, and I bit my lip to stop from bursting into tears. "Let me go, Reve."

Reve's hand disappeared, and I turned and ran towards the first demon I spotted. I told him to go home. He ran in the same direction I had seen the others run. This would work. I could send them all back to where they came from.

Things became a blur then. I had to clamp down on my fear every time I got close to a demon.

I had sent at least ten back when my command didn't work. The demon was humanoid and killed another angel right in front of me.

"What was that, little girl?" He cocked his head to the side and then lunged for me, grabbing me around the neck.

I felt my throat being squeezed as he lifted me off the ground and then threw me. A body caught my fall, and we landed in a heap.

The demon stalked towards me again, a murderous look in his eyes. Why hadn't my command worked?

"Go home! Kill yourself!" I sounded desperate. Was this it? Was I about to die because I was stubborn?

The body under me shifted and jumped to his feet. I looked up to see Reve. He grabbed two knives from somewhere on his body and met the demon head-on.

They were a blur of motion as they fought. I scrambled back a little farther, and then a head rolled towards me.

I shut my eyes, and for the first time in forever, I said a little prayer to the man upstairs to not let it be Reve.

Arms lifted me, and my eyes snapped open. Reve looked back at me. I was shaking and felt the overwhelming urge to cry.

Things hadn't processed up until that point. I slowly turned my head and looked around. There were so many bodies in the grass that the grass was no longer green. It was painted a dark brown color with both angel blood and demon blood mixing.

"We need to go, Danica. I know you want to help, but this is why we didn't want you here."

My eyes were drawn to a spot near the Astronomers Monument. Or at least what was left of it. The ground and air were rippling.

"Do you see that?" I pointed and stepped around Reve, heading towards it.

"See what?"

As I got closer, I could feel the change in the air. It was warmer and smelled like the inside of a drawer that hadn't been opened in years.

I was about ten feet away when several demons

came out of it and ran straight towards us. I raised my sword, but before I could get a swing in, Asher, Olly, and Tobias landed in front of us and killed the demons.

"How the fuck did she get here?" Asher moved towards Reve with a murderous look on his face. "We had a plan."

"She ran." Reve ghosted just before Asher got to him.

He turned towards me. "Let's go."

Olly and Tobias were fighting off another few demons that just came through the ripple.

"Is that a present?" Asher let go of my hand that he had just taken and approached a beautifully wrapped box near one of the beheaded demons. "Jesus. It has your name on it, Dani."

I stepped up beside him and looked at it. I squatted down and then snatched it from the ground. Asher made a noise, and I looked over at him.

"How do you know it's not a bomb?" I rolled my eyes at his question and ran a thumb over the name tag.

It was my father's handwriting, I was sure of it. I ripped it open and dropped the box as my fingers clasped the watch that was inside. It was one of his favorites that he always wore.

He was probably wearing it the night he was taken.

I gripped it in my hand, and before Asher could

grab me, I darted towards the rippling that was growing smaller.

When I had first spotted it, it had been the size of a garage door. Now it was no bigger than a regular door.

"Dani, no!" Olly jumped in front of me, right before I got to the doorway.

He pushed me backwards as arms came from the ripple, grabbed him, and pulled him back into it.

He vanished, and a loud pop shook the ground as the ripples seemed to close in on themselves.

I fell to the ground where it had been and ran my hands over the grass frantically. It had just been here. Where had it gone?

"Olly?" Asher yelled. He was standing in front of me and turned around in a circle with a confused look on his face. "Where the fuck did he go?"

"It was... I think it was where the demons were getting through." I grabbed grass in my hands and ripped it from the soil. "Fuck!"

"What do you mean?" Asher knelt next to me. "Is he..." He grabbed me by the arms and made me look at him. "Where is he?"

"He was pulled into Inferna." Reve appeared and bent down to pick up my father's watch I had dropped. "You two get back to the academy. Tobias and I will find Michael."

My eyes stung, and I wiped at them with my

forearm. I just kept fucking things up. I should have been the one pulled into Inferna, not Olly. It had all happened so fast.

The fighting seemed to be winding down as Asher silently scooped me into his arms. He was staring straight ahead, unblinking. I put my head against his shoulder as we shot into the sky.

Chapter Ten

*W*e landed back on campus in the empty parking lot next to our building. It was deafeningly quiet, especially compared to all the noises of fighting.

My stomach rolled, and I bent over with my hands on my knees. Asher put his hand in the center of my back and stood silent next to me. I dry heaved a few times and let the tears fall to the asphalt.

Ethan might be dead. Olly might be dead. It was all my fault.

Asher grabbed my elbow and pulled me up from being hunched over. He cupped my cheek with worry in his eyes and then headed for the door without a word.

I wanted to speak but didn't know the words to say.

I needed to be strong. I needed to hold myself together.

We got back to my room, our room, and I sat down on one of the mattresses on the floor. My resolve to stay strong was crumbling quickly as I watched Asher grab his bottle of whiskey. He took a very long drink from it and stood still, the bottle gripped in his hand.

I pulled my knees to my chest. I needed to say something. Do something.

Before I came into their lives, they had normal problems to deal with. Now, it seemed every time I turned around, I was causing another catastrophic problem.

I bet my dad wished he would have just let me fail at life. Now the entire angel population of Los Angeles was risking their second lives because I had been too eager to be away from the academy.

Reaching into my pocket, I pulled out my dad's watch. I rubbed my thumb over the face of it. It wasn't even working anymore. I set it on my knee and stared at it.

"Asher-"

"Fuck!" He hurled the bottle across the room. The thick glass of the bottle fell with a hard clunk to the floor.

I flinched, the watch falling off my knee and onto the mattress.

Asher went into the bathroom, slamming the door behind him. I heard the shower turning on and got up off the mattress to pick up the bottle that was lying on its side. With shaking hands, I put it upright on the table. A small puddle of whiskey lay on the hardwood.

I pulled my shirt over my head and mopped up the mess. I grabbed the bottle, walked to the sink in the kitchenette, and dumped the rest of the liquid down the drain.

I swiped at my face, wiping the tears that had fallen without me even realizing it, from my cheeks. I was so tired. Not just from lack of sleep, but life.

Looking at the room, I took in the mess that was my life now. Duffel bags lined a wall with clothes spilling out of them. The two mattresses lay in the center of the room, taking up most of the floor space. The sheets and blankets were crumpled and tangled.

I walked towards the bathroom, unhooking my bra and letting it fall to the floor. What was another piece of clothing left lying in the middle of the room? I didn't care. None of us seemed to care much for cleanliness these days.

After I pulled off my boots and jeans and left them by the bathroom door, I stepped inside. The door had at least been left unlocked.

I shut the door gently behind me and pulled the shower curtain open a bit. Asher was standing with his head bent, his arms leaning against the shower wall. His shoulders shook, and choked sobs escaped his mouth.

"Ash," I whispered, letting him know I was behind him.

I gulped back my own tears and stepped into the shower. Asher didn't move or look in my direction. I placed a hand in the middle of his back and put my chin on his shoulder.

He took several deep inhales and exhales. "We have to get him back, Dani."

"It's my fault. I didn't listen." I put my cheek against his back and wrapped my arms around him. "I'm always fucking up."

Asher didn't say anything as we stood there. He moved one of his hands to cover mine.

"When this is all over, I'll understand if you and the others want to-"

"Don't." He shook his head and then turned, so my head was on his chest. "None of this is your fault. You did what any of us would have done."

"But-"

"But nothing, Dani." He rubbed my back in small circles. "Olly has this theory that everything that happens is fated to happen."

I looked up at him. His eyes were blood-shot, and sadness was evident on his face, but his lips quirked a bit as he spoke about Olly.

"He thinks the cup is sentient, and it's pissed that the world is going to shit." He laughed a little. "Like it's seeking vengeance or something. I think it's a load of crap."

If Olly thought the cup had a mind of its own,

maybe it did. When I had stolen it for Lilith, it had seemed to be egging me on, daring me to take it. It could have just all been in my imagination.

"It's not that hard to believe that an inanimate object might be alive or something. There are demons, and hell is some sort of parallel realm. Plus, Reve is the rightful king of hell." A giggle burst out of me. It was crazy hearing it out loud. "You don't think he'll make us bow to him, do you?"

Asher kissed my forehead. "I'd like to see him try to make us. I'll make him kiss my left nut before I ever bow to his ass."

"Why the left one?" I looked down at the nuts in question. They both looked the same to me. "Is it the inferior nut?"

"The right is only for you." He kissed me gently and then grabbed the loofah and body wash.

We stayed in the shower for several more minutes before climbing out. Reve was sitting on the counter.

"Michael is here." He lifted his chin towards a stack of clothes on the closed toilet seat. "Figured since he already saw your bra and panties lying around, we shouldn't make him feel even more awkward."

"How long have you been sitting there? Is Toby all right?" Asher dried off and grabbed his jeans.

"He's fine." He hopped off the counter. "How do you know I haven't already kissed *both* your nuts? All those hands and mouths. The passion."

Asher paused in the middle of pulling on a tee-shirt. Reve grinned and then disappeared.

"Can you believe that fucker?" Asher finished pulling on his shirt and watched me as I got dressed.

"He's just trying to provoke you." They were all getting along better with Reve, but things still weren't perfect. Especially since Reve purposely said off the wall things to them.

I took a deep breath and then opened the bathroom door. It was time to deal with reality.

Michael and Tobias were sitting at the table. Both looked exhausted and a little worse for wear. Asher and I sat down in the other two chairs. Reve was sitting on the counter. That seemed to be his seat of choice.

"Is Ethan okay?" I looked at Tobias, who had a grim look on his face. He shook his head in the smallest of movements. "He's... he died?"

Michael sighed. "He no longer has his human form. A soul can only return to it once. He's with all the other souls."

My heart ripped in two. I didn't know how much more death I could handle. My heart hurt for Cora.

"A guardian angel knows the risks they sign up for when they make the decision to come back to Earth." Michael seemed to read my mind and gave me a sympathetic look. His words did nothing to ease the pain of losing a friend.

My gaze fell to my dad's watch that sat in front of Michael. I went to grab it, and he stopped me.

"It's a message. The date on it is set for two weeks from now." He rubbed his hands over his face and then picked up the watch. "But that was before Oliver got pulled through."

"What does Olly have to do with the date on the watch?" Asher leaned forward on his arms.

"If Lilith figures out that it's not just Lucifer's blood that can create a gate, so to speak, but any archangel..." He took a sharp inhale of breath. "It's probably more like a week."

"Wait. What?" I snatched the watch before he could stop me again and put it on my wrist.

"The whole concept of hell as a punishment for darkened souls was meant to be shared among the archangels. That was until Lucifer made one too many mistakes." Michael sat back in his chair. "Once we have him back with us, some things are going to change. They're going to be how they should have been all along."

"What if we can't save him before..." I choked on my words, and Reve came behind me and put his hands on my shoulders.

Michael was quiet for a few moments before he spoke. "Let's not think about that. You will. Archangels can never die, but grave injuries can take years to heal. The longest I've been down is two years."

My eyes went wide.

"Partial decapitation." His words were not helping at all. If anything, they made my anxiety over my dad and Olly being at the mercy of a deranged madwoman worse.

"So, what do we do now?" I cleared my throat and looked up at the four men staring back at me.

"We go to hell. They are expecting us."

Of course there was a welcoming party waiting for us.

IF MY FATHER had the choice, it would have been for me to never visit hell.

My visit when I was nine years old, wasn't because he *wanted* me in hell with him. What father would want his daughter to go to hell?

I had begged and begged for him to take me. I had an intense curiosity and didn't care if it was literal hell. Plus, when it's Christmas Eve, it's hard to say no to your nine-year-old.

I had been excited to finally see where my dad disappeared to all the time. As soon as my feet hit the ground in the foyer, a wave of pain washed over me. It had felt like my skin was being ripped off. Then I vomited all over my dad's expensive suit.

Needless to say, I didn't see much of hell.

As we stood in the backyard of my house in Montecito, I wondered why my dad never tried to take me again. Was it because I had gotten sick?

Was it because he had a wife and a houseful of little demon angel babies running around?

We all held hands like we were about to go on a field trip somewhere. There was popping in my ears, and then we were standing in a courtyard of what looked like a medieval manor.

My house was lined up directly with where Lucifer stayed in hell.

The sound of water trickling in a fountain nearby and birds chirping greeted us. Right along with the smell of a distant burning fire.

I looked around, taking in the large outdoor area we were in. Everything seemed darker here. Dark stones, dark sky, dark trees. There was at least a large moon to give some light to the landscape.

I squinted in the direction of the trees. "Are those birds?"

"Don't look at them! They will attack you." Reve stepped in front of me. "Let's just all not look at or touch anything."

"So, just assume everything is going to kill us?" Tobias took a step towards the fountain. "Jesus Christ, is this blood?"

"It's water. There are algae in the water here that turns it red. It's safe to drink." While I trusted Reve, I wasn't too keen on drinking water that looked like freshly spilled blood.

A man stepped into the courtyard from an outdoor hallway. He came to a stop in front of Michael and bowed his head. "Archangel Michael.

It is lovely to see you again. Are these the guests you spoke of?"

"They are. I trust that you have prepared for them?" Michael was all business. I wondered if he ever let his hair down and had a laugh.

"Indeed, we have."

The man looked up, and I had to bite my lip to stop a gasp from escaping. His eyes were almost entirely black, but other than that tiny little detail, he appeared human. His eyes landed on me first.

He took a step forward and held out his hand. I looked at Michael with raised eyebrows, and he nodded. The man took my hand and clasped it in between both of his.

"Not many know of your existence. It is an honor to meet you." He let my hand go, and then he spotted Reve. His eyes went wide, and he opened and shut his mouth like he was going to say something, but couldn't quite get the words out.

"Alex. It is good to see you again." Reve stuck out his hand, but instead of taking it, Alex dropped to a knee.

"We did not think you would ever return, my king."

Tobias snorted, and Alex looked up and narrowed his eyes as if he was offended at the noise.

"Please stand. There's no need for formalities." Reve shifted uncomfortably and looked at me.

I just smiled. What else was I supposed to do?

Information overload was a thing, and I was currently experiencing it.

A loud crack of thunder sounded in the distance, and Asher grabbed onto Tobias's arm. I was worried about what this was going to do to him. I didn't want my need for him to be at the detriment of what sanity he had regained. Without Olly around to soothe him, it was going to take all of us to help him hold it together.

He had refused to stay behind. I couldn't blame him.

"Let's get you inside and settled. We have many things to discuss." Alex rose from the ground and turned on his heel.

"Is he a servant?" Tobias whispered to Reve.

Michael cleared his throat. "Alex is an Incubi demon. He is currently in charge of our part of Inferna in Lucifer's absence."

Incubi demons feed off of having sex and the sexual desire they create. I looked at Alex with entirely different eyes now. Sometimes I wondered if I was the female version, a Succubus. I seemed to really like sex.

"What kind of demon is Lilith?" I wondered aloud.

We followed Alex through two massive iron doors and into a large living room. It looked unused. I doubt the devil ever had company. But maybe he did. I mean, how much did I *really* know about my dad? Would I ever get to know him?

"She doesn't have a classification. She slowly evolved into whatever she is. She was human at first." Alex stopped and turned towards us.

I stopped in front of the giant black stone fireplace and looked at my pictures lining the mantle. I had only just started to really get to know my dad. I blinked back tears as I felt a hand on my lower back.

"You were a cute kid." Asher pulled me towards him. "What happened?"

I spun and smacked his chest. "Thanks."

"I will show you to your rooms now."

Alex put us in two rooms that adjoined with a Jack and Jill bathroom. He said he would send for us in an hour.

I plopped down on the large four-poster bed and pulled off my boots. I needed a nap, especially if we were going to be traipsing through hell looking for my dad.

"Why does he even have a house like this?" I laid back and moved my arms like I was making a snow angel. It was the softest material I had ever felt. "Seems a bit excessive for just one man. Our house in Montecito isn't even *this* big, and it's pretty big."

"It's a symbol of his status." Reve walked to the velvet-covered windows and pulled the curtains back. The sky was a dark shade of blue, like it couldn't make up its mind if it were night or day.

"Didn't you mention a castle?" Asher was

looking through drawers. He was antsy, and I couldn't blame him.

"I did. It's much bigger than this place." He left the drapes open and moved towards the bed. "There's a storm coming. We'll have to wait until it passes to make our way towards where Lilith has your father."

I moved up to the pillow and shut my eyes. Reve settled in next to me and pulled me against him.

"How'd my dad save you?" I ran my fingers along his arm. He made a noise in his throat. "You said you locked yourself in your castle's dungeons."

"I did." He cleared his throat, and Tobias and Asher sat on the edge of the bed. "My powers were useless against her, and I still hadn't developed my phantom form yet. She sent me to kill him."

I stopped moving my hand and gripped his forearm.

"Clearly, I didn't succeed. Your father is strong. I don't think Lilith realized just how strong he is. He was going to kill me until Alex told him I was royalty. He gave me a drop of his blood, which broke whatever hold Lilith held over me and then took me to Earth. He saved me."

We lay in silence for several minutes before I let out a frustrated grunt and sat up. "Let's explore."

I felt like a little kid as we creeped out of the room and down the hall to the first door we came to. It was just another guest room. Most rooms off the hallway we were in were guest rooms with large four-poster beds.

"Did he ever have visitors?" I just assumed he existed a lonely life in hell. "He didn't have any friends on Earth."

"I'm not sure."

I crossed over into another wing of the house and opened the first door. It was a library. Finally, something other than beds.

Books lined the walls, and chairs were scattered throughout the room that was double the size of the large bedrooms. I walked over to an armchair that had a large book sitting on it.

"Widows?" I grabbed the book and flipped through it, stopping on a picture of a large group of women.

They looked human, but on the next page was a close up of one of them. Her eyes were nearly black, and her skin looked like it had spiders crawling under the surface. I scrunched my nose and goosebumps broke out across my skin. I hated spiders.

Reve grabbed the book and let out a small laugh. "Widows are the definition of female empowerment. They kill men that wrong women. I was actually surprised there was one in that mall the first time demons got through. They usually stick to themselves."

"There are only women Widows?" I made my way across the room to a shelf and scanned the titles. It seemed each type of demon had a book. Who had written all of them?

"Yes. Well, no. There are men, but they always wrong the women in some way and end up dead. They are a dwindling population... or at least they were the last I heard."

We set off down the hall and found where my father kept his watches. It was rather loud inside, with all the ticking.

"You know what this reminds me of?" Asher ran his finger along the top of a case. It looked like a jewelry store in the room. "That movie, *Hook*, where Captain Hook keeps all the clocks."

I slid the watch from my wrist and placed it in an empty slot in a case. Tobias put his arm around me and tucked me against him.

"I think I'm ready for a nap now." I leaned against Tobias.

What if we couldn't find him or get him back? I wasn't ready to lose my dad.

Chapter Eleven

Reve

*W*atching Danica try to hold herself together was painful. She put on a brave face, but we all saw through it. She was scared shitless.

We all were.

After she was asleep, we made our way downstairs. Michael had wanted to meet with us to come up with a plan. I didn't know how much of a plan was needed.

"Alex is preparing supplies for your journey. He says you won't be able to leave until after the storm passes." Michael laid out a paper map in front of us. I didn't want to tell him that we didn't need it because I knew exactly where we were headed.

"So the plan is to walk to this castle where they are keeping Olly and Lucifer, break in, and take them back? That seems a little too easy." Asher sounded skeptical as he looked at the map. He traced his finger over the path that was drawn from where we were located to the castle.

"Reve will do most of the breaking in. He knows the castle well."

I grunted. There was a secret entrance I could get us through, although Lilith might have changed the place in the centuries I had been gone.

"Lilith needs to be taken out." Michael looked at each of us. "At all costs. Can you handle that burden?"

"Do you mean..." Tobias stood up straight and crossed his arms. "I thought our job was to protect Danica."

"Yes." Michael looked sad. "I know you are willing to risk your own lives, but sometimes protecting the ones you love means letting them go."

"Fuck." Asher put his face in his hands. "She should be part of this conversation."

It was quiet for several minutes. Danica should have been here, but I was grateful she wasn't. She didn't need to know we were discussing killing her mother and the possibility of one or all of us dying in the process.

Or the possibility that she might die too.

"She'd go to Heaven. Right?" I looked at Michael, who now wore an impassive expression.

"Yes." His expression was grim, and he looked

at Tobias. "It will be similar to dying in war. She'll remember that she fought in one, but not the specifics."

Tobias sat down in a chair and looked at Asher. "So, she won't remember us?"

"It's hard to say how much will be blocked from her memory. I'm not privy to that information."

We couldn't let her die.

MORNING CAME TOO QUICKLY. We made our way downstairs to the dining room for breakfast. This might be the last regular meal we'd get for a while.

Food in Inferna was similar to Earth, except the animals and plants were a bit different. Several servants brought out our food and drinks.

"Your Highness, if the food and beverages are not to your liking, we can get you something else." A servant placed a plate with eggs, bacon, and toast in front of me.

I didn't need to eat, but it was something to occupy my time and to feel more a part of the group. Danica was already devouring her eggs.

"Good?" I took a bite of bacon.

Everything here had richer flavors. It might be home to demons, but they took care of the land and its resources.

"It's delicious. There are chickens here?"

"They are similar to chickens." I wasn't about to tell her they had ten eyes and ate the males.

Inferna was savage like that.

But the bacon was top notch.

"Your Highness, would you like more bacon?" I looked up at the servant, and she bowed deeply.

"I'm fine. Thank you."

"Your Highness." Asher set his fork down and took a drink of his coffee. "I just don't see it. Toby is more kingly than you."

Danica sniggered and hit Asher's arm. "He's kingly in the bedroom."

"So, what you're saying is that he's a better lay than us?"

Danica nearly choked on her juice. "You are all kingly in the bedroom."

"There is only one king. Asher is more of a princess." I smirked.

Tobias cleared his throat. "Are you planning on reclaiming your throne?"

I picked at my eggs. If we were able to take care of Lilith, the throne would be up for grabs. Did I want it? I couldn't see myself staying in Inferna where the sun never shines, and the air always smells faintly of burning wood.

"I've been on Earth for so long because I never wanted the throne to begin with." I set my fork down. "I might have to settle things, but I plan on returning to Earth. That's where my home is."

After breakfast, we gathered the packs Alex

prepared for us and headed out to where a carriage was waiting for us. It was too risky to fly and way too risky to take air transport. Lilith would see us coming from a mile away.

We climbed into the horse-drawn carriage, settling in for the first part of our journey. The carriage would take us to the edge of the Black Forest, and then we would go the rest of the way on foot.

As soon as we started rolling along the dirt path, I solidified.

"What if we get there and she controls you again?" Danica was peeking out the window. She looked in awe of what she was seeing, which was a whole lot of dark landscape.

"It will be more difficult for her here. She could do it before because I was young. In Shanghai, she could because I am weaker on Earth."

I had kept many things from them. Including the fact that Lucifer had offered to help me get my throne back, and I had opted to live on Earth.

"What can you do now that we're here?" Tobias had been quiet since we left Earth. I could tell he was worried.

"At the height of my father's power, he could cause visions in entire villages. Lilith used me to do the same, but on a much smaller scale since I was still developing my skills."

"Can you give Lilith visions and dreams?" Danica looked at me and frowned. "If so, you should give her a vision of me cutting off each finger one by one and then shoving it down her throat."

My eyes widened at the violence in her voice. Surely she was joking. I shook my head in response. Lilith's brain was utterly inaccessible to me. Whatever kind of demon she had evolved into over the centuries was a strong one.

She would have to be if she was able to get back and forth to Earth. I thought only archangels were capable of such feats. That and a dose of dark magic and angel blood.

We fell into a comfortable silence. The first leg of our journey would be smooth. This part of Inferna wasn't very populated, which was why the angels had set up their prison of souls here.

The carriage came to a stop after several hours. I went to my phantom form before the door was opened. Lilith probably thought I was dead, and I intended to keep it that way.

We climbed out, and Asher, Tobias, and Danica took their packs from the demon that had driven the carriage.

We walked through the Black Forest at a snail's pace. Any faster and we would attract attention. The Black Forest lived up to its name. The trees were black, and the low light that was ever-present in Inferna made everything look dark blue.

It looked like it should be freezing, but the temperature was warm. At night, the air became chilly, which was the only way to distinguish night from day.

It was approaching nightfall when a pack of creatures came at us from the side. I sent a vision at them, but they continued forward. They relied on their other senses instead of sight.

"What the fuck are they?" Asher had ahold of Danica's hand and let it go to unsheathe his sword.

All of the creatures' heads turned in his direction at the sound.

"They're like zombies." They weren't exactly zombies. You couldn't turn into one from a bite, but they did enjoy feasting on the flesh.

"Can I try to get them to go away?" Danica looked to Tobias.

I don't know why she was asking permission all of a sudden. She tended to do what she wanted. Not that I could blame her. Tobias nodded.

"Leave us alone."

They stopped and then turned around and headed back the way they had come. It was an amazing thing to watch but it made me shudder.

We continued on. About an hour later, we came to a small group of tents surrounding a campfire. If demons had set up camp, they were most likely humanoid.

"Stay here." I didn't know if whoever was living in the woods were friend or foe. My family had a lot of pull in Inferna, but there were a lot of demons that hated our power.

The campsite was occupied but whoever was living there wasn't there at the moment. I turned back towards the group and froze. They were walking towards me with their hands in the air and a group of about ten men behind them.

"Let us go." Danica was attempting to control them. From this far away, they looked humanoid, which seemed to be harder for her to control since demons that took human-like forms usually had much more complicated brains.

"They don't smell right," one of the men said.

I floated around the group. I breathed a sigh of relief that they were shifters. I could deal with shifters.

I landed in front of them and revealed myself.

"Holy shit. Is that-"

"It can't be."

"Wait until-"

They all started talking at once, and Asher, Tobias, and Danica darted behind me while they were distracted.

"Enough!" I yelled.

They fell silent but kept their knives and clubs raised. None of them looked familiar.

"Are you back to save us from Lilith?" One of the men took a step forward, and one of his buddies put out his arm and stopped him from getting any closer.

"Something like that."

"Please join us tonight. It would be an honor to

host you and your party," one of the men offered with a slight bow of his head.

I looked over the men and decided they seemed sane enough. Shifters struggled to hold back their emotions, so if they meant to harm us, they would have already.

We set up our own tent next to theirs and gathered around the campfire. They had just been out hunting when they came across us.

"You don't live in your village?" I asked as I watched Danica bite into the leg of the boar they had killed. She let out a small, satisfied groan.

"She kicked us out centuries ago. Instead, demons who do her bidding live there. Anytime we set up somewhere new, she takes that from us too. Many packs moved North."

Leaves crunched behind us, drawing everyone's attention. The shifters sniffed the air and then went back to eating and drinking. Someone was coming, but they didn't seem to think it was a threat.

"Reve?" The feet stopped behind us.

I stood and turned to look. I'd recognize Alaric's voice anywhere. He was just as I remembered. Short dark hair, scruff on his face, shockingly green eyes. The eyes of an alpha.

The eyes of the man who was supposed to be my guard.

I walked towards him and stopped before him. My heart wanted to leap out of my chest, and I swallowed down the lump that had worked its way into my throat.

Then I punched him.

"REVE?" Danica unzipped the tent and crawled inside.

She laid next to me on her side and reached for my bruised hand. She ran her fingers across the knuckles.

I turned my head and looked at her. "He was supposed to protect me. Instead, he ran."

"He would have died." She brought my knuckles to her lips and kissed them. They would heal all the way soon.

I shut my eyes. "I thought I was over it. I guess I was wrong."

"Did he really have a choice? I mean, he would have been killed."

I looked back at the top of the tent and sighed. She was right. Of course she was right. But Alaric had taken a vow to protect me until his last breath. Running from his own last breath didn't exactly show his loyalty.

"He was your best friend, right?" I grumbled my response. "You haven't seen him in practically forever. He could help us."

"I don't trust him."

"I didn't say you had to trust him." She kissed me lightly on the lips and stood.

I followed her out of the tent and sat next to her and Asher around the fire. It was starting to get cooler, and the warmth felt nice.

I looked at Alaric across the fire, and he stared back at me with a bruised cheek. He hadn't dared to take a swing back at me, although I had seen the desire to strike me back in his eyes.

He stood and sat on the ground in front of us, his back to the fire.

"I'm sorry. I was young and scared and-" A small squeaking noise interrupted him, and he looked down at the pocket of his jacket.

The tiniest head poked out.

"What's his name?" Danica leaned forward to get a better look at the monkey. If it could even be considered one. It could fit in the palm of Alaric's hand.

"Picard Rupert Ferdinand the Fifth."

"That's a fucked-up name for a tiny little pipsqueak." Asher snorted and reached his hand out to pet the little guy. "Ow! Fuck!"

Asher shook his hand and examined the small bite.

"He doesn't like being called names." Alaric held the monkey in his palm and stroked the top of his head. "Isn't that right, Picard?"

The monkey rubbed its little head, which was

no bigger than a golf ball, into his finger. It made a tiny squeaking noise as if it were talking to him.

"I thought those things hated wolves."

I watched as it jumped off his hand and scurried across the fallen leaves to my pant leg. It scampered up and sat on my thigh, looking at me with a cocked head and glossy eyes. I held out my hand, and it climbed onto it and then curled into the tiniest ball. It was the cutest thing I'd ever seen.

"I'm not most wolves."

"Wait. You turn into a wolf?" Asher was leaning forward with his forearms on his knees. "There are vampires *and* werewolves? I'll be damned."

"Don't mention those bloodsuckers in the same sentence as wolves." He let out a growl. "But, yes. All of us turn into something. Some of us are wolves. Foxes. A squirrel."

He gestured to the other men.

"How does that work? Being a squirrel shifter? Is your monkey a shifter too?" Danica was fascinated with the new information. I could see the wonder in her eyes.

"We recognize each other as pack. Picard is not a shifter. He is the last of his kind, unfortunately."

The conversation died down after a bit, and Danica stifled a yawn. I could tell she wanted to stay awake and learn more about this realm, but we all needed to recharge for what lay ahead.

We made our way to the tent, and the three situated themselves in the sleeping bags.

I first noticed that Tobias and Asher were weakening when we woke up after our first night in Inferna. I'm not sure they realized it themselves. There was a reason that archangels were the only angels that could get in and out.

Inferna drained turned angels.

Eventually, they would weaken to the point where they wouldn't be able to fly, heal, or whatever else it was they could do.

I sat at their feet in the tent. It had taken Asher a while, but he had finally stopped tossing and turning.

I licked my lips as I watched his eyes move under his eyelids. I could feel his unease. His restlessness. I looked over at Tobias and Danica entwined together. Tobias never showed signs of nightmares. Recently, Danica had less severe nightmares.

I knew that with their weakened states, I could push into both of their brains and into their dreams. But did I want to?

Asher kicked out a leg, and I flinched as he came close to kicking Danica. Maybe just once wouldn't hurt.

I moved to hover over him and pushed into his dream.

"If I never have to eat another damn K-ration again, I'll be a happy man. I don't even need pussy ever again. Just give me some damn meatloaf and mashed potatoes!"

Laughter went up around Asher in what looked like an abandoned warehouse.

Tobias was next to him and stuck a cigarette in his mouth, lighting it up. "I can't wait to eat my wife when I get back."

More laughter. I looked around the group of men. They looked ragged, like they had just gotten done on the battlefield.

All of a sudden, a loud explosion rocked the building, and a mortar shell crashed through the center of the roof, exploding on impact.

Panic ensued, and Tobias and Asher jumped to their feet. The men on either side of them were wounded.

"Go get litters!" Tobias had jumped into action and was applying pressure to someone's leg that had nearly been blown off.

Asher took off out of the building and down the hill. I followed. He ran to a medic camp and collected stretchers. I could feel his panic and fear, but like Danica, instead of feeling energized by it, I felt drained.

Tobias was coming down the hill towards Asher, and someone yelled, "Watch out!"

Asher dove over Tobias and a mortar shell hit the ground and exploded, sending debris everywhere.

I made my way up the hill and grabbed Asher's hand, yanking him out of the hell he was living in.

We landed at a miniature golf course. As soon as I released his hand, he shoved me.

"Where's Toby?" He looked around frantically. "Toby!"

"He's fine. He's safe."

Asher grabbed the front of my shirt and shoved me against a large, decorative boulder.

"We have to go back and get him! We can't just leave him there! He'll die!"

I'd never experienced this before with Danica. He was still freaking the fuck out. I tried to reign the control of him, but it wasn't working.

"Calm down, man! I'll go get him, okay?" I didn't know what the fuck I was saying.

I tried to make Tobias appear, but Asher had taken over the dream himself. His pupils were pinpricks in his irises as he looked around again. His grip loosened a bit.

"You'll bring him here too?" His hands shook as he held onto my shirt.

"I'll get Danica too. Just... stay here and don't freak out."

I walked away from him and took several deep breaths. I had never attempted to merge people into dreams together before. I knew my father could do it, but before he could train me on the finer points of it, I had killed him.

I floated above them in the tent. Asher had rolled away from Danica and curled into a tight ball, fisting the sleeping bag covering him. I didn't want to move him, so I laid down in the small space between them. I put my hand over hers and a hand on Asher's back.

She stirred but didn't wake. Tobias snored softly and tightened his grip on her. I focused on all three brains and pushed in.

My head spun as I grabbed Tobias out of his

dream, which had an awful lot of sex going on, and Danica out of hers, which had her lying on a beach somewhere. I was somewhat surprised she was having a good dream for once.

At least, that's how it appeared. Knowing her dreams, some kind of monster would come out of the water and try to eat her.

I landed with Tobias and Danica at the miniature golf course again to find Asher sitting against the boulder he had shoved me into with his knees drawn to his chest.

"I brought them. See?" I approached him, and he looked up. He looked like hell, with bloodshot eyes.

I offered him my hand, and he took it.

"What is this, Reve?" Danica stepped towards Asher with concern etched on her features and then took him in her arms. He buried his face in her neck.

"Regular angels are weakened in Inferna. I could get into his nightmare. I had no clue they were that bad."

"Toby?" Asher finally pulled away from Danica and looked at Tobias. "Are you okay?"

"I'm fine." Tobias grabbed Asher and pulled him into a hug, smacking him on the back. "Which one was it this time?"

"The warehouse."

"Damn." Tobias sighed and put his hands on Asher's shoulders. "I'm sorry."

Danica disappeared and then reappeared with putters and golf balls. "Let's knock some balls around."

I kept a close eye on Asher as we moved through the golf

course. He seemed to relax more and more, but I still felt like he was in control of the dream instead of me.

"You're staring at me." Asher turned towards me after taking a putt through a moving obstacle. "I'm fine now."

"Are you? If you were, you'd loosen up a bit more." I set my ball on the tee and hit it through the spinning blades of the windmill. It sailed through with no problem. "We need to wake up soon."

I was nervous that I wouldn't be able to wake the three of them up with Asher in control. I didn't even know how he was holding onto control like he was.

"Maybe we shouldn't wake up." We walked along the path behind Tobias and Danica. He had his hand in the back pocket of her jeans. "At least here we're safe."

"Our minds are safe. Our bodies are lying in a tent in the middle of Inferna with a crazy-ass demon woman sitting in power."

"Then why don't you go and take care of her. I'm sure you can get the drop on her with your invisibility. You watched us for over a month, and we never even knew."

"You make me sound like a creeper."

He turned and grinned at me. "You are *a creeper."*

"Fuck you, Asher." I shoved his arm and caught up to Tobias and Danica. "We need to get him out of here."

"But he's so relaxed now. A little longer?" Danica slid her arm around my waist, and I shut my eyes.

"If we stay any longer, you might get stuck here. Like, be in a coma kind of stuck."

"That wouldn't be a bad thing, would it?"

Fuck, they were all spiraling now.

This had been a mistake. The only way I could think to get them out was to turn the dream into a nightmare. The little control I had still only extended to the environment.

I stood in the center of the path and looked at them. "I'm sorry."

The ground exploded around us.

Chapter Twelve

Danica

I woke with a scream and nearly butted heads with Tobias, who was breathing heavily. Everything had been fine, and then the explosion happened. It had felt so real.

Asher.

Sobs shook his body. I placed a tentative hand on his back, and he jerked away from the touch.

"Asher... sweetie. It's okay. We're okay." I tried a hand again, and this time he didn't cringe at my touch.

"I'm sorry. I'm so sorry." Reve was standing up, slightly hunched over so his head wouldn't hit the ceiling of the tent. "I thought-"

"Get out, Reve." Tobias sat up and glared at him. "What the fuck were you thinking? He isn't Danica!"

"I thought-"

"Get out before I throw you out."

Reve looked at me with pleading eyes. I wasn't sure how to feel about the whole thing. On one hand, he had really fucked. On the other, he had been trying to help Asher, not hurt him.

But that explosion.

He disappeared before I could say anything. Tobias ran a hand over his face and let out a shaky breath.

"Jesus Christ. What the fuck?" Tobias moved closer to Asher and me. "Are you okay?"

I nodded and moved my hand in small circles on Asher's back. He was still shaking, but his sobs had stopped. What *had* Reve been thinking?

"He shouldn't have been able to do that." Tobias put his hand on Asher's shoulder.

"We wouldn't let him end the dream." Asher shook his head. "The fucker didn't have to make an explosion, though."

"I'll go talk to him." I ran my fingers through my hair the best I could, and then pulled my hair back into a ponytail. "Is it even daytime? I can't tell."

The sky was still dark, but it was slightly warmer than before we went to sleep. I climbed out of the tent and spotted Alaric stirring something in a pot over the fire.

"Have you seen Reve?" I joined him next to the

fire and held my hands out over the flames. For being hell, it was a little on the cold side.

Alaric looked at me with furrowed brows and then laughed. "I doubt he'd show himself around me."

"We need to leave soon, and he disappeared." I hugged my arms around myself.

"I was talking to a few of my men last night. We'd like to help you." He scooped some of what looked like oatmeal into a bowl and handed it to me. "At least until you get to the castle."

"I don't see why not. You know your way around here better than we do."

"Plus, your angels are weakening."

"Excuse me?" I paused halfway to my mouth with a spoonful of oatmeal. "What do you mean they're weakening?"

"I'm a predator. I can sense a weakened animal. Even last night, I could smell them weakening." He started eating his food while walking away. "Let them know they can help themselves to breakfast."

I turned and walked back to the tent. At least now I understood how Reve could get into their dreams.

WE SET off about an hour later. Alaric and three of his men joined us. Reve hadn't returned, no matter how much we called out for him. He had to be staying invisible to avoid us. There was no way he would leave us.

"It should take a few hours to get to the castle. Once we're there, there's a secret entrance we can use to get you inside." It was hard to take anything Alaric said seriously because he had a miniature monkey on his shoulder.

"We appreciate you helping us since Reve left us high and dry." Tobias was holding my hand as we walked.

Asher grunted from the other side of me and looked straight ahead. "I just want this all to be over."

I sighed. I wanted it all to be over too. For so long, I had wanted to experience hell for myself, but now that I was here, I missed Earth.

Alaric stopped suddenly, and Picard made a small squeaking noise. Before Alaric even had time to react, a dart hit him in the neck. He turned slowly towards us before his eyes rolled back, and he collapsed in a heap.

The other three men were hit with darts and fell as well. Picard was jumping up and down on Alaric's chest, making really loud screeching noises for such a small creature.

Tobias and Asher pulled their swords and put me in between them. We looked into the trees but didn't see anyone or anything.

It would have been a good time for Reve to appear. Just as I had the thought, ten men dropped from the trees in front of us. We backed up several steps as they fanned out into the forest.

I pulled a knife from my belt and threw it at one of the men. It hit him in the shoulder, and even from the distance, I could see his eyes turn black.

"Oh, shit." My body was screaming at me to run, but instead, I pulled out another knife and prepared to fight.

Darts came whizzing towards us, and Tobias spread his wings and took them in his left one. He winced and fell to the forest floor, his wings retracting as he fell.

"I'll fight them off. Run." Asher took a step forward and dodged a dart.

I hesitated for only an instant before I took off back towards the campsite. I could only hope that none of the demons had managed to circle around. I zig-zagged to avoid any darts aimed my way and felt like I was making progress when arms went around my waist.

I screamed as I was lifted off the ground and thrown over a shoulder. My knife was still in my hand, so I swung my arm and stabbed the demon in the back. He laughed and turned back in the direction I had just come from.

"Bring them all." He spoke sternly to the other men as we passed through the area where Alaric and his men, Asher, and Tobias were lying on the ground.

"Where are you taking us?" I grabbed onto the

knife and pulled it out. There was no blood, and his wound closed instantly.

"Your knife does nothing to me, young one." I stabbed him again. "You can stab me all you want."

"Where. Are. You. Taking. Us." I made sure to annunciate each word in case he didn't understand me. I squirmed, and his hand pressed more firmly into me as he carried me in the direction of the castle.

"There's a bounty on your head. Her Highness said you'd be in this direction. She wasn't wrong."

A motherfucking bounty? How had she even known we were here? Did Tobias's suppression not work anymore?

"Whatever she's offering you, I can pay double." I tried to pull the knife out again, but it was stuck in his back as if he was holding it in.

I really couldn't pay this demon, but he didn't need to know that. It seemed like the thing to say. I didn't know how smart these demons were.

He grunted, and the knife fell out of his back and to the ground before I could catch it. "My whole life, I have dreamed of having a place at the castle. I don't think you can top that."

"I don't understand."

His deep baritone laugh shook me as we walked. "You really are from Earth, aren't you? I didn't believe it when I heard it. Queen Lilith's daughter, a human."

"I'm not a-" I stopped as we came out of the

trees, and a castle rose up in front of us. "There really *is* a castle. Holy shit."

Sometimes when someone tells you something exists, you don't believe it until you see it with your very own two eyes. The castle seemed to rise out of the ground and looked exactly like a castle straight out of a fairytale.

This was no fairytale, though.

I should have been fighting more, trying to escape, not gawking at the castle. We entered what appeared to be a small village until we came to a stone building with bars for windows.

"You will stay here until she fulfills her end of the bargain." We entered into what was definitely a jail.

He set me down in a cell, and the others put Asher and Tobias in with me. They were still knocked out cold from whatever was in the darts. Alaric and his men were placed in a cell next to us.

"Let us go."

He laughed again and shook his head. "We aren't idiots, young one. Your tricks don't work on us."

The demon who had carried me and one of the others stopped at the entrance of the jail and stood facing each other. They were having a hushed conversation, and then, all of a sudden, they turned to stone.

"What the fuck?" I squinted, trying to see better. There was some light in the cell, but not much.

The stone figure slowly turned its head in my direction, and its eyes turned red. I backed up, and it swiveled its head back towards the other.

I was going crazy. I sat down against the stone wall and shut my eyes, hoping that when I reopened them, I'd be back to reality, and two gargoyles wouldn't be holding us hostage.

I STOOD outside Reve's door and knocked for the fifth time. Where was he?

I moved to the window and peeked in. I could see the pristine white countertop of the kitchen, and that was it. He was ignoring me or wasn't home.

"I'm going to steal your bike! You better open up!" I knocked one last time before making my way to his crotch rocket. He could fly. It seemed like a useless toy.

I threw my leg over it and sat on the leather seat. It was a sexy-looking bike.

"That's a good look for you." Reve appeared next to me and gave me a small smile. "I like to see you with your legs spread."

I grinned and leaned forward. "I bet they'd look even better wrapped around you."

He made a noise in his throat and moved onto the bike seat behind me. His lips brushed the shell of my ear. "I'm going to get you out of here, Dani. I promise."

"You left." I sighed as his lips moved down to my neck, and he breathed a sigh against my skin. "Why'd you leave?"

"I was scared you wouldn't forgive me."

He placed his hand on my thigh, and I covered it with mine. "I'm sure Tobias would have kicked your ass, but then they would have forgiven you. Eventually."

He pulled me back against him and wrapped both arms around me. "I have to go get reinforcements. My abilities don't work against the demons in this village. They are using a rare herb called Tutela. That also means they are even more dangerous because they are truly Lilith's followers."

"Please hurry."

"I love you, Dani."

I turned, and he kissed my cheek before vanishing.

MY EYES FLUTTERED OPEN to find Asher staring at me. His eyes were bloodshot, and a crease had formed between his eyebrows as if he had been thinking too hard.

"Reve?" he whispered.

I shifted on the floor and winced as my tailbone protested sitting on the hard ground. I nodded.

"I can tell when he's in your head. You get this look on your face like you're... home." He looked at me thoughtfully. "I think that's how I felt when he was in my head. That's why I didn't want to leave the dream."

I scooted closer to him and wrapped my arms around him, putting my chin on his arm and looking up at him. "It can be addictive. Escaping in the dreams."

"What did he say?" Tobias stretched his arms over his head and then stood. He was looking around the cell as if it was suddenly going to have a weakness in the bars.

"He's going for reinforcements," I whispered. "Alaric said you two are weakened here. That's why Reve could get in your head and how Lilith knew where we were."

"Fuck." Asher ran a hand over his face and shook his head as if he couldn't believe it.

"Do you think Olly is weaker here too?" Tobias sat down on the other side of me.

I shrugged. "My dad isn't. At least I don't think he is. If he was, how could he have so much control over the demons he works with?"

"They used to be human." Alaric's sleep-filled voice came from the other side of the bars. "Humans are weak from what I know of them."

Picard climbed out of his jacket and scurried over to our cell. As if to prove Alaric's point, it jumped up onto Asher's thigh and then chomped down on his finger.

Asher was about ready to whack it clear back to Earth. Before he could, I picked it up between my thumb and forefinger.

It let out a flurry of squeaks as I held it by the back of its neck like it was a cat. "You are a bad monkey!"

Its little eyes welled with tears, and its tiny lip quivered. Jesus, why was he so cute?

I put him back down, and he ran to Alaric's open palm on the ground.

"Can't that little shit break us out of here or something?" Asher glared at Picard. Picard turned around and spit his tongue out. "He has a fucking piss-poor attitude."

"The last man that spoke poorly of Mr. Ferdinand had his dick bitten off in his sleep." Alaric scratched Picard behind the ear. I laughed as Asher put his hands over his dick.

"I can't believe I'm sitting here watching a demon wolf shifter talk to his pet monkey." Tobias ran his fingers through his hair and rubbed the back of his neck.

A silence fell over us as the reality of our situation grew bleaker. Alaric confirmed that the two stone men at the entrance were gargoyles. Even if we could make it out of the cells, the gargoyles would stop us from leaving.

I leaned against Asher and ran through the last several months. When I had punched John in the face, I would have never thought my actions would lead me to being stuck in a musty and damp cell in hell.

"What if it's one big giant nightmare?" I was playing with Asher's fingers. His head was back against the stone wall.

"Not all of it has been a nightmare. Has it?" I

felt Tobias shift next to me. His hand slid behind me to rest on my hip.

Alaric looked over at us with curiosity written in his eyes. He hadn't said anything in a while. None of his men had.

"For everything bad that has happened, there has been twice as much good." Asher looked down at me then shut his eyes. "The bad has just been really fucking bad. You think we're all a dream in your head?"

I made a noise in my throat. The thought had crossed my mind several times, especially when shit got pretty dicey. If it was a dream, it was pretty elaborate. Maybe I was in a coma?

"Reve wouldn't do that," Alaric practically growled.

Tobias leaned forward and looked at him. "He exploded our dream the other night. He tortures people in their dreams. Or at least he did before Danica."

Alaric moved closer to the bars and wrapped his hands around them. "She's his mate."

Asher's eyes popped open, and he rolled his eyes. "We don't believe in that kind of shit on Earth."

"That's a shame." His face became thoughtful. "You're all mates. How does that work with three men?"

"There's four," I said. "It works how you think it would."

He let out a whistle. "They just share you? Don't they fight?"

I laughed, and Tobias squeezed my hip. "They fight, but over time it's become less frequent. I don't think that sharing me is an appropriate explanation of what we have together."

"She's always protected and feels loved. But we also feel the same way from her and each other. I'm pretty lucky. I not only get Danica but also three best friends." Tobias kissed my temple.

My heart swelled, and a smile tugged at my lips. The feeling was short-lived.

The two gargoyles at the entrance transformed back into men and stepped to the side. Tobias jumped to his feet and stood in front of me.

I peered around his legs as the two goons that seemed to be Lilith's right-hand men, came and stood in front of our cell.

"Mark. Sam. I see you still don't know how to think for yourselves." Alaric stood, and one of the goons stepped over to his cell.

They stared at each other before a growl ripped from Alaric's throat, and the goons looked away. Alaric and his men laughed at whatever had just transpired.

"You're the one locked in a cell right now. What do you think, Mark? Will Lilith let me be the one to take his head?"

"Sure. As long as I can eat his monkey in front

of him first." He gestured for one of the gargoyles to unlock our cell. "She wants the girl only."

Tobias hadn't budged from his spot in front of me. Asher rose to his feet as well, and together they stood as a united front.

"Are we going to do this the easy way or the hard way?" one of the men said, stepping into the cell.

Tobias brought his fist back and swung at him. He moved faster than I could track and grabbed Tobias's fist before it connected with his face. A grin spread across his face, and his fist connected with the side of Tobias's head, sending him to the hard stone floor.

I rushed to Tobias, who was unconscious on the ground. Asher stood clenching his fists at his sides but didn't strike.

"Now, are you going to come with us, or do we need to knock this one out too?"

I stood and squared my shoulders. "Go away."

They both threw their heads back and laughed. "That shit doesn't work on us, princess."

I would have taken his name for me as an insult, but I guess I literally was a princess. I looked at Asher. I couldn't get a read on what he was thinking, but there was a tick in his jaw.

"What will happen to them?" My voice was surprisingly even considering how scared I felt at the prospect of seeing my mother again.

The last time I had seen her, she had poisoned

me and then stabbed me in the chest. She wasn't exactly mother of the year material.

"They stay here. Lilith will decide. You think you have a choice in this matter? You don't." Sam or Mark, I'd already forgotten which one was which, stepped forward and grabbed my elbow.

Alaric and his three friends growled from the other cell. Picard was on Alaric's shoulder and let out a screech.

"Get your hands off her," Asher warned. I had never heard him sound so menacing before.

"Asher." I put my hand on his arm and looked at him. "There's no use in you getting hurt too."

I looked down at Tobias, who had rolled over and let out a pained groan. I knew I didn't have a choice. I just had to hope that Reve would come through for them.

"She's a smart one, this one." They laughed again and stepped back out of the cell.

I turned to Asher and wrapped my arms around him. "It will be okay. Reve is coming." I didn't think anyone except him heard me. The goons were back to glaring at Alaric.

I knelt down next to Tobias and put my hand on his cheek. His eyes cracked open before shutting again. I hoped he could still heal himself.

Before I lost my courage, I stood and walked out of the cell.

Chapter Thirteen

 t crossed my mind several times to run. Now that I was walking on my own two feet and not slung over a gargoyle's shoulder, that plan was quickly squashed.

We were in a small village near the castle. The houses were made of stone, and the streets were dirt in some places and cobblestone in others. I felt like I was walking through medieval London.

Many demons came to their doorways or stopped in the streets to gawk at me. Most looked human. *If* I ignored their eyes and the extra appendages some had.

"Do all demons live in towns?" I was walking between Tweedledee and Tweedledum. Had I tried to run, their big meaty hands would have stopped me in an instant. I'd given up trying to remember their actual names. It didn't deserve the extra mental effort.

"No. Only the civilized ones." I didn't even want to know what uncivilized demons were like.

I snorted at his answer, and he turned his head to glare at me, his eyes seeming to glow. "And what are you?"

"Civilized."

"No. I mean, what type of demons." I scanned the surroundings, looking for a place to escape to. Nothing looked promising.

"Bear shifters." He grunted and grabbed my elbow, steering me towards a paved set of stairs leading up a hill.

I hated stairs. I also hated hell and demons. Except for Reve. Unless Reve really had ditched us. I hoped he was just laying low until the time was right.

"I don't understand how Inferna and Earth are so similar." I was thinking out loud because I was trying to ease the panic churning inside my gut.

"Inferna was a fuck up. He took what he liked and started over on Earth."

"God?" I was half-angel, and most of the time, I doubted one man was behind creating everything. It would certainly explain how eerily similar I was finding certain aspects of Inferna, though.

"Is that what he calls himself?" They laughed, and one of them prodded my shoulder. "Speed up. We don't have all day."

We came to a large iron gate that slowly opened to let us into a courtyard. The gate shut with a clang, and I felt my freedom slowly getting farther and farther away.

My dad was inside the castle. At least if I were going to be held against my will, it would be with my father. Hopefully, Olly was inside too.

I couldn't think about what state I would find them in.

I followed the two men up to a large iron door, and we waited. A small piece of the door slid open, and an eye peered out at us. It felt very much like *The Wizard of Oz*, except I wasn't going to be going back to Kansas.

The door opened, and a tall man stood to the side in a suit. He bowed his head slightly and gestured with his arm to enter. I looked to my two captors, and they pushed me forward and into the dark foyer.

If it could be called a foyer. It was big enough to house a family of four and had a large chandelier hanging in the center that sparkled unnaturally.

"We'll show you to your room. You will have a few hours to bathe yourself and dress for dinner." One of them took the lead and went to a large staircase that took my breath away.

"So you aren't sticking me in the dungeons? How kind of you. Can I also find my father and boyfriend up here?" Tweedledum stopped on a stair and looked down at me. Maybe it had come out a little too snarky.

I couldn't exactly fight two bear shifters with my

fists, so my words were my next best weapon. Except that all of my words were mostly just nervous banter to keep from losing my shit.

"You have quite the mouth on you for being in the situation you're in."

"Well, I am the daughter of the evil demon queen and the devil. What did you expect?"

He made a noise and continued up the stairs while Tweedledee followed. We entered a long hallway and stopped in front of a pair of double doors.

"This will be your room. We will be right here outside the door. The windows are locked." He opened the door and waited for me to walk inside before shutting the door behind me.

I heard the lock turn and immediately ran to one of the windows. I checked them all, but they were all locked with bars covering them. Of course, escaping couldn't be as easy as they made it in the movies.

My attention was drawn to a chair where a flowing pale blue gown was laid out. There was a card on top.

MY PRINCESS,

At last, we can be together as a family. Please wear this dress to dinner. You can find the accompanying accessories on the dresser.

Love,

Mom

I THREW up a little in my mouth and chucked the card across the room. The dress had way too much taffeta and far too many embroidered flowers for my liking.

I looked down at my dirty clothes and lifted an arm to sniff. I didn't seem to have a choice about what I was going to wear. I'd have to suck it up and dress like I was going to prom.

I MUST HAVE ALREADY BEEN EXPERIENCING Stockholm syndrome because I had no problem pampering myself in the large bathtub. I dressed like the princess Lilith wanted me to be and completed my look with a thin crown of diamonds on the top of my head.

At least I thought they were diamonds. For all I knew, they could be melted together souls of kidnapped puppies.

I looked at myself in the floor-length mirror and tried to put on a fake smile. I was going to have to get Lilith to believe I was all for being a happy little family.

A fist pounded on my door before the lock was undone, and the door opened. I followed the bear shifters down to the main floor, where we entered the dining room.

I stopped in my tracks.

"Danica. So glad you could join us." Lilith stood at the head of a long table. She gestured to the seat to her right.

My breath caught in my throat as I looked at my dad. He had cuffs around his wrists and neck. It didn't appear they were attached to anything.

I made my way to the seat to her right and sat down. I didn't take my eyes off my father, who was now staring at me from across the table. Lilith sat down and tapped her nails on the table. I looked at her.

She looked exactly as she had in Shanghai. Her mahogany hair was pulled into a chignon with tendrils of hair framing her face. Her eyes shined with mirth, or maybe that was just the crazy in her leaking out.

"Tomorrow evening, there will be a ceremony to reunite our family." She took a sip of her wine and then grinned at me. "You, my dear, will be bound to me as my one and only heir."

A lump formed in my throat. "And my dad?" I choked out.

"We are already bound. We were sorry that you had to miss it. It really was the party of the century, wasn't it, sweetheart?" She patted his hand that was balled in a fist on the top of the table. "Now that we are bound together, if anyone hurts or attacks me, he feels everything." She laughed in that way that sent chills down my spine. "Isn't blood magic wonderful? I can't wait to teach you!"

I'm pretty sure if I had a mirror, I would have been pale as a ghost.

I looked at my dad, who sat to the left of Lilith. He stared straight ahead, his jaw set in stone.

"Your father already made the mistake of trying to kill me after the ceremony while I slept. He won't dare make that mistake again. Isn't that right, sweetie?" She put her hand over his and squeezed.

"Right," he bit out through his teeth.

She cleared her throat. "Honey. I don't think I like the tone you are taking in front of our daughter."

I bit my tongue to stop myself from saying something utterly stupid. The whole exchange made me want to vomit. She was fucking crazy. How was it that I had come from her womb? Would I eventually end up like her?

She stood from her seat and snapped her fingers. The two goons approached the table carrying a knife and the Holy Grail. My eyes nearly popped out of my head, seeing it.

I pushed back from the table, and my dad looked at me and shook his head. I grabbed onto the edge of the table as Lilith took my dad's hand, swiped the knife across his wrist just above the cuff he had on, and let his blood fall into the cup.

"It will be any day now when the barrier will

finally give way and stay open permanently." She tapped a nail on the side of the cup as it filled with his blood. "It's unfortunate that your boyfriend seemed to have skin of steel this time around."

"Olly? Where is he?" I choked out.

She threw her head back and laughed. "In the dungeons. He's a fighter, that one. If only John were still around to make his special serum to weaken him." She made a noise like she regretted killing the doctor. She lowered the cup to the table and wrapped a cloth napkin around my dad's wrist.

"How can you touch it?" I nodded towards the Holy Grail.

"It bends to my will now. If an angel tried to touch it while here, it would burn them." At my confused expression, she continued, "It pulls its power from whatever power source is greatest. Here in Inferna, it is an object of great darkness."

The servants returned to the table and cleared our plates. Lilith remained standing and grabbed the goblet.

"I will leave you two for a few moments while I take care of this blood." She sauntered out of the room with the goon squad behind her.

The doors shut, and I heard a lock click into place. I stood and rushed to my dad.

"Dad-"

"You shouldn't have come." He put his palms on the table and stood, the bloody napkin falling to the floor. His cut was nearly healed but should have closed already.

"We can't let demons get through. We have to stop her."

"There's only one way to stop her, Dani." He ran his hand through his hair, and I noticed the puckered skin of scars running across his forearm.

I grabbed his arm and pulled it towards me, running my thumb over the pink, raised skin. "What has she done to you?"

He sighed and looked forlorn. "She weakened me and then bound us together. You can't let her do it to you. These cuffs prevent me from breaking free. You need to find a way out of here. Where are your guardians?"

"In a jail." I whimpered and brought the back of my hand to my mouth to stop a sob from escaping. "I don't think they're coming."

He shook his head and then sat back down in his chair. I sat in the chair next to him.

"You have to kill one of us." He spoke in a barely audible voice. He straightened in his chair and then turned towards me.

My eyes widened. "What?"

"Our lives are tied together. Kill one of us, you kill the other."

Did he even hear what he was asking me to do? I couldn't kill someone. I couldn't even kill a spider.

"There has to be another way. I can't just-" I felt

myself starting to panic and wanted to jump up and run from the room.

"Yes, you can."

Tears slid down my cheeks, and I shook my head. He took my face between his hands.

"You can. You must, or she's going to permanently open a way to Earth. She already managed to get the barrier open for a substantial amount of time. And if I did manage to escape, she would go back to kidnapping angels. In large quantities, their blood can get a single demon through."

A sob left me. He pulled me towards him, smoothing my hair back.

"Find something sharp. Stab it through my heart. Right here." He took my hand and put it over his chest. "Stabbing me is your best bet."

"Dad. You can't die. I can't-"

"This is the only way. She thought binding us together would protect her. She won't see this coming."

No words were coming from my mouth. Instead, I was inhaling sharp gasps of air. Kill my father? I couldn't. I wouldn't. There had to be another way.

He brought my hand to his cheek, and I looked back at the dull gray eyes that should have been smoldering. He was weak. I was no genius when it came to reading angels, but the power that once coursed through my father had significantly diminished.

"Tobias, Reve, Asher, and Oliver." He let out a shaky breath. "They will protect you and keep you safe." I opened my mouth to argue with him, but he shook his head. "Sometimes, life isn't fair, Danica. I can think of no other way to go than saving you." His voice cracked, and a tear slid down his cheek.

"I can't."

He leaned forward and kissed my forehead. "You can. Tomorrow at the ceremony before she performs the ritual."

I was about to respond when the doors opened, and Lilith strode back in, looking smug.

"I love you, Danica," my dad whispered.

"I love you, too." I hugged him tightly before the goons took me back to my room for the night.

Chapter Fourteen

Tobias

*M*y head was throbbing from the blow I took to the side of the head. It should have been healed in less than five minutes. Inferna really was weakening us. How could we protect Danica if we were completely drained of what strength and abilities we had?

I turned on my side and curled into a ball. I was a poor excuse for a man. They took Danica. They took Oliver. Now we were locked in some musty smelling cell with gargoyles guarding us.

My job was to protect, and I failed. It wasn't the first time I hadn't protected my loved ones. I allowed a moan to pass through my lips. My vision grew fuzzy, and I passed out for what seemed like the hundredth time.

"Margie." I stood at the entrance to the kitchen, my hands shaking.

She had been cooking my favorite meal: pot roast with mashed potatoes and green beans. I shut my eyes and breathed in. The aromas usually caused my mouth to water and my stomach to growl, but tonight it just made bile rise in my throat.

We knew it might happen, with the news of Pearl Harbor and the president calling for war. But I thought, no, I prayed, that there'd be enough voluntary enlistments to stop the ever-present fear of my serial number being called.

"Dinner's just about ready. Can you get the boys washed up?" She didn't turn around. She was busy mashing potatoes.

"Margaret."

She stilled over the stove, the potato masher dropping into the pan. I never used her full name. The last time I had used it, I had been down on one knee, asking her to marry me.

She turned slowly, bringing her hand to her mouth as she took in what I could only assume was my scared-shitless expression.

"We'll hide." A tear slid down her cheek, and she came to me, grabbing my face between her hands. They were warm and smelled of potatoes. "We'll pack up the car and head to Canada."

I shook my head and put my hands over hers. A sob left her, and I put my forehead against hers.

"I have to do my duty. Even if I don't want to." The words felt foreign. As much as I loved being an American, I wasn't sure the price for that was worth it now that I had the choice to fight ripped away from me.

I had thought about enlisting with the news of the attack, but I had a family. Now that I had been one of the unlucky ones selected, I didn't have a choice.

My wife was well off. Old money. She didn't need me to support her. There was no way they were letting me out of it.

"What if-"

"No what-ifs. I probably won't even leave American soil." I cupped her face and searched her eyes for the strength I knew was there. "It will all be fine."

I jolted awake as something wet ran up my face. Picard was licking my tears. I batted him away.

Who the hell has a pet monkey? PETA would have a field day over it. As if seeming to know that's what I was thinking, Picard spat his tongue out at me and ran back to Alaric.

I didn't know what to make of the wolf shifter. He seemed decent enough, but he had also left Reve to be captured by Lilith. I didn't trust him.

I pulled myself up and leaned against the wall next to Asher. He looked like shit. I'm sure I did too.

"When you enlisted, how did your wife react?" I tried to steer clear of war talk with Asher. It was hit or miss whether it would cause him to spiral. Lately, he had been sharing a lot more of his memories.

He shrugged. "How do you think she reacted? She called me a selfish asshole, smacked me, and then let me fuck her on the kitchen table. Why are you asking?"

"Why does everything have to be so crass with you?"

"What would you prefer I say, Toby? That I made love to her on the kitchen table?" He made a noise in his throat. "It is what it is. I'm not going to sugarcoat the terminology because you're a pansy-ass."

I rolled my eyes and looked over at him. He was clenching his jaw.

"I remembered when I told Margie I had been drafted. It's the last memory I have before leaving." I sighed. It must have been painful for me to leave if I couldn't even remember the day I left.

He grunted and turned his head to look at me. "We weren't the only ones that fought in that war, were we?"

I shook my head. Our families might not have been in the line of fire, but every time the mail came or a knock sounded on the door, I'm sure they felt like they were in a battle of their own. I shuddered, thinking about Margie opening the letter announcing my death.

"I honestly try not to think about Lena. It hurts too much." I was surprised he mentioned her by name. He rarely spoke of her. Even when we served together, he didn't talk about her.

"Did you ever find out what happened after we... you know..."

He shook his head in response. I had always assumed he had taken it upon himself to track her down and find out what she did after his death.

"It might help to know."

"I don't want to know if another man was sticking it in her, Toby. You might be into that shit, but I would have probably killed the fucker, even though it was my fault I died."

I decided to keep my mouth shut. He was getting agitated, and the last thing we needed was to come to blows.

"I think Reve is here," Asher whispered after several minutes of silence. "Don't ask me how I know that, but I've started being able to feel the fucker lately."

I looked around the cell, and my eyes stopped in the corner. I could sense him too if I really focused. I wondered how recently that had started happening.

He wasn't saying anything. I didn't exactly trust him at the moment, what with the whole dream fiasco and him up and leaving. It was a shame because I had started to actually like him enough to want to hang out.

Alaric grunted and stood along with his men. They were a relatively quiet bunch. I half expected shifters to be loud.

"They're coming." Alaric scooped Picard off the floor and put him in his pocket. I should have asked what kind of demon he was. Surely he was some-thing other than just a miniature monkey.

"Who's-" Asher's question was interrupted by loud thumps outside.

I looked in the direction of the gargoyles who

had just started to transform back into men when two massive fists came smashing down on top of them.

Not going to lie. Asher and I ended up clutching each other like two little girls watching a horror movie. The building we were in shook and rubble fell from the ceiling. Asher was shaking, so I kept hold of him.

"Tony. That's enough!" Reve's voice was coming from outside the bars now. "Stand guard."

An eye appeared in the doorway and looked in at us. Its pupil was big enough that I could walk into it. Jesus Christ. I was about to pass out.

"I'm surprised you found Tony. He and Miles have been MIA for centuries." Alaric was at the bars with his hands wrapped around them. Hair was sprouting from them like he was mid-shift.

I was an angel, but seeing different types of demons I had only read about was making me question everything I knew about the world. I mean, hell, we were in another realm that literally meant hell in Latin.

Reve appeared and grabbed a set of keys among the remains for the gargoyles. I guess with strong enough fists, even gargoyles could be defeated.

He unlocked our cells. "Invitations have been sent out to the elite demons, requesting their presence at a coronation ceremony this evening."

"What?" I knew I sounded stupid asking the

question, but I was still mind-fucked over the giant that was still staring at us with its eye in the doorway.

"There was a coronation months ago for Lucifer. She's going to bind Danica to them and make her the heir to the throne."

"But you're the rightful heir." Alaric stepped out of the cell and took several breaths. The hair, or fur, on his hands disappeared.

Reve ignored his comment and looked at me. "I'm sorry."

"You're late." I led Asher out of the cell and eyed the giant. "Can you move your friend here."

"I have an army waiting in the forest."

I stopped and blinked at him. How he had managed to round up an army of demons in less than twenty-four hours was beyond my comprehension. But then again, he was King Reve, not just pain in the ass Reve.

"I have a plan." Reve stepped in front of us to stop us from leaving out the door. The giant had luckily understood my comment and moved.

"And what's that?" Asher was pale, but at least he was talking. "If it involves any more explosions, I'm out."

"We'll sneak in through the secret entrance that appears to have been abandoned since my days in the castle. It will easily give us access to the dungeons."

"What if they aren't in the dungeons?"

"Then, tonight, we'll go to the coronation."

"Lilith is going to know we're up to something. You can't miss a big ass giant and an even bigger hell serpent." Alaric stepped beside Reve.

"She doesn't have as many demons on her side as she thinks." He got a faraway look in his eyes as if he remembered something from the past. He had quite the history to remember. "I will need to stay invisible. Someone from inside the castle told me that she thinks I'm dead."

"Why would she think that? You're indestructible." Alaric seemed shocked that Reve would think he wasn't immortal.

"Not on Earth."

We left the building, and the sight greeting us was destruction. It was as if the giant had just barreled right on through the center of town. Waiting on a pile of rubble from a building was a hell serpent that was twice the size of the one we had seen in Shanghai.

"This way." Reve was invisible again. He was headed to the right of the castle. In fact, we were moving farther away from it.

We walked in silence. Alaric was in front. He seemed to know exactly where Reve was. He had to be smelling him or something. I tried to sense Reve like we had in the cell, but there were too many other stimuli to distract me.

We ended up at the edge of the Black Forest and went into the tree line. I was starting to wonder where this secret entrance was when we came to a rock formation. It was covered in black moss, but if I stared long enough, I could see the opening.

"I'm not going in there." Asher had stopped and crossed his arms.

I honestly didn't want to go into the dark cavern either, but we didn't have a choice. I put my hand on Asher's shoulder and gave it a reassuring squeeze.

"Do we have any lights?" Our cellphones had already died, so using their flashlights was out of the question.

Alaric's men slipped through the opening, and he stopped, reaching into his pocket for Picard.

"We don't need light to see in the dark. Here. Take Picard. He will help." I put my hand out, and Picard jumped onto my hand and then up my arm to my shoulder.

"How is a monkey going to help?" Asher rolled his eyes. He just didn't like the little guy because he bit him. I would have bitten him too if he had made fun of my name.

Alaric shook his head and followed his men.

"Picard is a luminous demon monkey. If you want him to, he will light up." Reve's voice came from just inside the entrance.

I looked at Picard on my shoulder and raised my eyebrows. A monkey that lit up? I didn't know whether to be scared or in awe. I slid through the entrance, and Picard made several noises before his entire body lit up like a magical orb.

"It's possible we are going crazy." Asher stood next to me, and we looked around the cave we were standing in.

The cave wasn't large but sloped downward towards a corridor.

"Reve, why are you still invisible?" I made my way carefully to the passageway where Alaric and his men had stopped to wait for us.

"She might have spies down here," Alaric answered for him.

A chill ran down my spine. We made a single file line and walked for what felt like ten minutes. One of the men at the front of the line held up his hand to stop us.

Before I even knew what was happening, Alaric and his men hunched and then dropped down out of the passageway. I caught a flash of fur and sharp teeth before several thuds and groans.

Picard seemed to vibrate on my shoulder before the light he was giving off disappeared, and we could only see a very faint sliver of light in front of us.

"It's a small drop, and then you need to crawl." Reve's voice came from behind us. "They will have taken care of any guards."

I could see Asher's eyes watching me as I crept forward and then jumped down into the hole. It wasn't as deep as I expected. What I wasn't expecting was to have to army crawl under rocks that looked like they could come crashing down at any second.

I made it through and stood in a dim hallway that was lit by torches. I felt like I was in the middle ages.

I put my hand out to help Asher up. He was holding it together well, all things considered. We took off in the direction of growls and turned the corner to find a large room with cells lining the sides and wolves dismembering demons.

As soon as I saw the pile of white, silver-flecked feathers in one of the cells, my heart stopped beating. The only thing that brought me back to the present was Asher grabbing onto my arm and squeezing it so tight that I thought he was going to rip it off.

"Do you feel it?" Asher whispered.

I looked at him, still frozen in place. Oliver was curled in a ball in the corner of the cell. His wings were wrapped around him, but there were large patches of feathers missing. One wing seemed to be at an odd angle.

"Feel what?" I grabbed onto his fingers that were digging into me and peeled them off.

"I have to take him."

Asher moved forward, stepping over an arm then a torso. The cell was locked, and I looked around for a set of keys. I grimaced, finding them clutched in a ripped off hand.

I grabbed them before I had time to talk myself out of it and unlocked the cell. Asher rushed in and scooped Oliver into his arms.

"I have to take him home." He blinked a few times and then looked at me. "It's like I'm being summoned, but it's a fuzzy connection. How am I supposed to get back to Earth?"

I looked down at Oliver, who had cracked his eyes open. Dirt caked his face, and his lips were drawn in a grimace of pain.

"Wouldn't let them take my blood," he mumbled. "They rebreak them every thirty minutes. They'll be back soon."

My stomach was in knots as his eyes closed again, and Asher looked at me with panic written in his eyes.

"Have to stop her." Oliver's head fell against Asher's chest.

"I'll help them get out of here," said one of Alaric's men, who had shifted back to looking like a man and not a beast.

"I can't just-"

"Go, Asher. If you are being summoned back to Heaven, you can't fight it." I looked down at Oliver's limp body, then back at him. "If you're with him, I think you can just fly straight through. Let the summons happen; it will guide you home."

He blinked a few times, and then his eyes glossed over. Danica had described to us what it looked like when Oliver and I had been summoned to take Asher back to Heaven. It was a chilling effect to see the blank stare on Asher's face now.

I watched them exit the room, feathers falling from Oliver's wings. I gritted my teeth and turned around in a circle, taking in the room. I wanted to vomit.

"This way." Reve's arm appeared and grabbed my elbow. "We'll go up through the servants' quarters and hide in a room there."

We made it into an empty servant's room, and Reve shut the door behind us.

"Some of the servants are going to get us tuxedos for tonight. It's the easiest way to have access to both Lucifer and Danica at the same time." He started pacing in front of us and looked out of sorts. "I tried to go find them the other night, but as soon as I get to a certain spot, my invisibility doesn't work anymore."

"Dark magic," Alaric grumbled from his spot on the floor. He had one of his men with him; the other two had gone with Asher and Oliver.

"That's an actual thing?" I sat down on a chair and put my elbows on the table, running my hands over my hair. I was ready to go back to Earth.

"How do you think you exist with all your special abilities? That's light magic. Inferna once was full of light magic." Alaric seemed annoyed to have to explain things to me. "It's only a matter of time before your precious Earth turns into another Inferna."

I looked at Reve with raised eyebrows. He just nodded and sat down on the mattress. It made a horrible squeaking sound underneath him.

"Me making an appearance will cause an uproar. Lilith will be distracted, and so will her guards. That's when you need to get Lucifer and Danica out." Reve looked between Alaric and me. "I don't know if Lilith will be able to control me. So be quick."

"What about you?" I frowned at him from across the small room. "She'll kill you."

Reve shut his eyes for a brief moment before opening them. His jaw ticked. "She'll die trying."

Chapter Fifteen

Danica

My day had been a blur of preparations for my coronation, or whatever it was that Lilith was calling it. To me, it felt more like I was heading to my execution.

I had been massaged, waxed, primped, and put in my room to select my gown. I stared at the ten dresses in front of me. I was not a gown person, but I couldn't help but drool over the beautiful fabrics and colors.

I grabbed a champagne-colored halter that was an A-line style and had intricate beadwork. I needed to be able to move in it. I also grabbed a pink ballgown that had a lot of tulle under the cupcake-like skirt. I hung both on the back of the bathroom door.

I hummed to myself and grabbed a lamp off the nightstand, and took it into the bathroom. I needed a weapon, and since there was absolutely nothing around I could shank someone with, I was going to have to improvise.

I shut the bathroom door and shoved a towel in front of it. I wasn't sure how good bear shifter hearing was, but I wasn't going to take any chances.

I turned on the shower and the faucet to drown out any noise. Grabbing a hand towel and the lamp, I looked at the mirror. My best bet was probably a corner.

I held the towel the best I could and then slammed the bottom of the lamp repeatedly into the glass. Pieces fell onto the counter.

I turned off the faucet and shower and listened at the bathroom door. All was quiet on the other side.

I smiled to myself. My plan might actually work.

I took one of the shards of glass and wrapped it in toilet paper and began ripping long lengths of tulle from the pink dress. I then tied the pieces together.

I wrapped the pointiest piece of glass I could find in the tulle and then tied it to my shin. It felt awkward, but that was the only place I could think of that had easy access and no body parts that would accidentally be stabbed.

Satisfied with my concealed shank, I slipped on

the champagne-colored dress. It was time to save the light from the dark. At least, I hoped this would be it.

I STOOD at the top of the staircase leading into the ballroom. I had been here before during my first dream with Reve. I looked around the room of sharply-dressed demons. Most looked human. I wasn't one to be fooled.

Several heads turned in my direction as I wiped my hands on the sides of the dress, smoothing out unseen wrinkles. I could feel the weapon strapped to my leg. Hopefully, it was secure and wouldn't fall off before it was time for me to make my move.

I moved down the stairs, feeling like I was on display. I suppose I was, being the daughter of their crazy queen. Were all these demons on her side freely, or had they been brainwashed into supporting Lilith?

I reached the bottom, and my dad stepped beside me.

"You look beautiful." He took my hand and set it in the crook of his arm. "Just remember to breathe."

I nodded and let him lead me onto the dance floor. He took my hand in his, and I put my head on his shoulder. Now would be the perfect opportunity to do what he asked and kill him.

"I'm proud of you, Danica Marie. I don't think I've ever told you that." I could only hear his voice, despite the room that was filled with music and chatter. We were in our own little bubble. "I should have been around more."

I shut my eyes and willed myself not to cry. "I love you, Dad."

When the song ended, he wiped the few tears that had escaped away from my face. Then he led me to a dais at the front of the room. Lilith was already sitting in one of the chairs, a crown perched on her head.

"My daughter, how beautiful you are tonight." She gestured to a chair to her right.

I took my seat and looked around the room. If I didn't know we were in Inferna, I would have never guessed the room was full of demons.

I was just about to excuse myself to the restroom so I could get ready to attack when I saw Tobias at the perimeter of the room. I grabbed onto the arms of the chair.

Lilith noticed him as well. She snapped her fingers, and two men grabbed him by the elbows and dragged him across the room.

I looked wide-eyed at my dad, and he shook his head. Lilith stood and walked down the five steps where the men with Tobias stopped and shoved him to the ground.

"Where are the rest of you?" She sounded angrier than I had ever heard her sound.

With all attention on Lilith and Tobias, I reached down and took the piece of glass out of the makeshift holster I had made. I held it next to my leg, waiting for the perfect moment.

I knew that whatever I did to Lilith would hurt Lucifer, but it surely couldn't kill him. He was an archangel. Archangels were indestructible. At least, that's what I kept telling myself.

I continued to reassure myself as the guests parted with hushed murmurs and gasps. Reve was walking towards us, and the room went silent.

No one moved to stop him, not even Lilith's guards. They all seemed to be in some kind of trance. Where were Olly and Asher?

"Boy, what do you think you are doing? Stop this madness immediately." She pulled a long dagger from one of the guards near her when her command didn't work.

"What's wrong, Lilith?" Reve had a deadly glint in his eye.

She straightened her back and stepped back up the steps. I stood and prepared myself. She was so focused on Reve that she wasn't paying my dad or me any attention.

I glanced over at my dad, and he nodded his head. He mouthed, "I love you."

I didn't want to do it.

I lunged towards Lilith, just like I had practiced in training at the academy. At the same time my shard of glass dug into her neck, she turned, and the dagger she was holding went into my side.

I'm sure a scream came from my lips, but I was in shock. The room suddenly came to life as Reve lost control of whatever he was doing to the demons.

I fell to my knees as Lilith pulled the dagger out and stabbed me again. My dad was on his knees, crawling in our direction. A flash of black fur flew over us and took out one of the goons that had been going for my dad.

My entire body felt like it was on fire as the dagger was pulled out for a second time. Or maybe it was a third time. She reared back again to stab me, but then her face froze in a scream as something hit her from behind.

She fell down the stairs as her body was engulfed in flames so hot that it felt like my own skin was burning.

My eyes landed on my dad. His hands still had tiny flames on them as he collapsed forward.

"No!" I scrambled as fast as I could on the blood-covered marble floor to him. "Dad!"

I rolled him over and put my ear near his mouth. He wasn't breathing. I collapsed back on my ass. The rest of the room was in chaos.

Bring him to me. The voice entered my head, and I looked around, thinking someone was talking to me. I was hallucinating from the blood loss. And the grief. The grief was making it hard to breathe.

I coughed and felt like I was about to pass out. I had been stabbed way too many times in my short life.

I barely even felt the pain anymore. I was going numb. It was the end of the road for me.

Bring him to me. The voice was more commanding this time. I looked up at the ceiling. It sounded an awful lot like Morgan Freeman.

I needed help.

I pushed myself to my feet and stumbled a little. How was I supposed to get my dad somewhere when he weighed way more than me?

I looked down at my wounds. My dress was now crimson. A laugh bubbled out of me at the sight.

I fell forward as a sense of peace washed over me. I caught myself on my hands and knees and felt the air stir around me. I turned my head.

Wings. One of my angels was here to take us. I smiled as the wings moved.

Bring him to me.

I looked at my dad and wrapped my arms around him.

"Danica! Wait!" I could hear Tobias, but I couldn't bring myself to pay attention to him.

My sole focus was on my dad.

The wings beat with more force, and I felt myself being lifted into the air. My dad felt abnormally light for being a grown-ass man, and I wrapped my arms around him tighter just in case.

I shut my eyes as we flew towards a window and broke through. I don't know where my angel was taking us, but wherever it was, I knew I'd be safe.

Chapter Sixteen

"*D*anica." The deep voice sounded in my ears, and I groaned. *Not again.* "It's time for you to wake up."

My eyes fluttered open, and I took in the white room that was the last place I wanted to be. What had happened? Was I actually dead this time?

"Where am I?" I sat up and took in my crisp white gown. I knew exactly where I was.

"Judgment."

I stood and looked at the ceiling. If this was judgment, then I was screwed. I had just played a part in killing my own mother. My eyes went to the diamond-encrusted door.

"So, this is it? If it opens, then I'm an angel, and if it doesn't..."

"It will open. You've always been an angel. Your father's angel."

I laughed and wanted to cry at the same time. *My father.*

"Is he... alive?" A tear slid down my cheek, and I sat back down on the bed. "He did this fireball thing, and then he stopped breathing."

The voice made a sound in his throat and then cleared it. "He threw most of the light he had left at her. He is recovering at the celestial hospital."

"Aren't I supposed to lose all my painful memories?"

"Do you want to lose them?"

I walked towards the door and put my hand on the handle. "I don't want to forget all the good."

The room went silent, and I bit my lip as I turned the handle. I half expected it not to turn, but it did, and the door opened into a very brightly lit hallway. I stepped out, and the door slammed shut behind me.

The hallway was long, with several doors. I walked towards what looked like an elevator. I tried a few doors along the way out of sheer curiosity, but they were all locked. Were there dead people inside? What happened if they died and the door didn't open?

I pushed the up button since there was no down button. The doors slid open, and I stepped inside. Every surface, including the floor, was encrusted in what looked like diamonds.

This was not what I had expected. I actually

wasn't sure what I expected, but everything covered in diamond-looking stones wasn't it.

I pushed the only button and looked closer. I wasn't a diamond expert, but they sure did look real. That or someone had too much fun with a Bedazzler.

The elevator ride seemed to go on forever. I couldn't help but giggle over the fact that the elevator was going up. Did the hell elevator go down?

The door dinged and slid open to a large white room that was filled with chairs and people. As soon as I stepped out of the elevator, there was a ticket dispenser.

"You have got to be kidding me." I pulled one out.

B102.

I looked up at the ceiling where a number was displayed. They were on A24.

Maybe they would be faster than the DMV. One would hope, with it being Heaven and all.

I made my way to an empty seat next to a little old man, who immediately turned to me.

"Oh, dear." He shook his head and clucked his tongue. "Too young. Too young, I tell ya."

I raised my eyebrows. "It was for a good cause."

"You remember? I don't remember a lick past my ninetieth birthday." His eyes went wide, and he shook his head again. "Whoooooeeee. I can't believe I made it to the pearly gates."

"You had pearly gates? I had a diamond-encrusted elevator."

In response, he burst into laughter and slapped his leg. Why had I never spent more time talking to senior citizens? They were hilarious.

I smiled, and his face softened. "You remind me of my great-granddaughter."

My smile fell, and I looked away. I had never experienced an actual family before. No doting grandma that let me eat popsicles before breakfast. No grandpa to take me on adventures in the backyard.

He reached for my hand, and I let him take it in his soft wrinkled one. "It'll be all right, dear."

I sure hoped so, because my heart was bruised and battered enough.

I'M NOT sure how long the wait was. Time seemed to function differently in Heaven. Not once did I feel hungry or that I had to pee.

B098 flashed on the ceiling, and my kind-hearted old man of a seatmate, whose name was Jack, stood.

"That would be me. Take care of yourself now, you hear?"

I smiled and then bit my lip nervously, waiting for my number to flash on the ceiling. Was this the part where they told me how much darkness my soul had and how long it would take to get my wings? I needed to get back to Earth.

I tried to look back over my shoulder at my shoulder blades but wasn't flexible enough. They had been slightly tingly since I sat down. I figured it was all in my head.

This whole thing might have been all in my head.

B101 flashed overhead, and I shut my eyes and took a steadying breath before standing. There was a single white door on the far side of the room where people had been knocking and gaining entrance.

What if this was some kind of social experiment to see who were followers?

I glanced around the room, and there were no other entrances. The elevator even had disappeared and just was a giant glowing area on the wall that people walked out of.

I approached the door and knocked softly. It opened, and I walked inside to find a desk and two chairs. I sat down and waited.

And waited some more.

There was a whole lot of waiting going on. My stomach should have been doing somersaults or churning up some bile, but instead, I felt oddly at peace. I could see why so many chose to stay in Heaven.

The door opened, and I turned. *Holy shit.*

"Brooklyn?" I stood, and she smiled back at me.

"Holy shit!" I smacked a hand over my mouth. "Crap, I don't think I'm supposed to say that here."

She laughed and sat down across from me, opening up a laptop she had. I didn't know whether to be in awe over the fact that she was sitting across from me looking better than ever or the fact that laptops seemed to work in Heaven.

I guess if cell phones worked from Inferna, then MacBook Air having a stronghold in Heaven wasn't so much of a stretch.

"I would say I'm happy to see you, but I'm not." She reached her hand across the desk, and I took it. "I mean, I'm glad you're *here* and not *elsewhere*."

I laughed. "I had my doubts."

She typed on the laptop, and her eyes widened. "It says here you already have your wings. But that can't be right."

She typed lightning fast and then looked at me, her eyes wide.

"What?" I looked over both my shoulders. "I think I'd know if I had wings. Wouldn't I?"

"I would think so. But this definitely says you are an archangel. Your trajectory is Los Angeles Celestial Academy, Class I, year two." She turned the laptop so I could see the screen.

"Bull shit." I pulled the laptop towards me and stared at the screen that had my picture, date of birth, date of death, and the information that said I was an archangel.

"What am I an archangel of? Fucking up?

Surely this is just Morgan Freeman's way of playing a joke on me."

Brooklyn gave me a confused look and then pulled the laptop back towards her. "There is a flag on here." She double-clicked on something, and I waited as her eyes scanned the screen. "It says instead of sending you to the Earth entry point, that I am to take you to the hospital to see your dad, Oliver, and Asher."

I gripped the arms of the chair and fought off the panic that was churning in my gut. "What's wrong with Olly and Asher?"

She shook her head and shut the laptop. "It doesn't say. If they're in the hospital, that's a good thing. That means they're healing."

She stood, and I jumped up. She walked around the desk to the same door we had entered and opened it. It led right outside.

I shouldn't have been surprised, but I was. I could deal with glowing monkeys, cotton candy-smelling gremlin-lookalikes, and even shapeshifters. Throw a door that opened to somewhere different than before, and I was flabbergasted.

"I'm not tripping out on acid, am I?" I followed her out the door and stopped. "The ground. Is it clouds?"

She laughed and looped her arm through mine. It looked like Earth, except everything was clean and shiny. The ground felt a little like the recycled rubber they put on playgrounds.

"Welcome to the Great City."

I looked up in awe at the tall skyscrapers that appeared to go on for miles and miles into the sky. I had no concept of what Heaven would be like, but it definitely wasn't what I was seeing. Where were the cute little cherubs floating on clouds?

Walking with Brooklyn, a sense of peace washed over me again. There weren't many angels walking or flying around, so it was quiet. We didn't walk far before we were at one of the giant skyscrapers, and I followed Brooklyn inside.

"This is where I leave you." She gave me a hug and pressed the button for the elevator. "It will take you straight to the floor the hospital is on."

I hugged her. "Will you ever come back to Earth?"

She gave me a sad smile and shrugged. "I don't think so. Take care of yourself. Tell Cora I said hi."

The elevator doors slid shut and began its ascent. Soft harp music played over the speakers, and I snorted. I shouldn't have been laughing. I was dead. My dad and boyfriends were in the hospital.

The door opened, and I stepped out to a reception area. "I'm here to see Lucifer, Asher Thorne, and Oliver Morgan."

The woman at the desk looked up from her computer and smiled brightly at me. "Ms. Deville! It is such an honor to meet you!"

She stood and took my hand in hers. I raised a

brow but followed her down the hall. She opened a door and led me inside.

"How is he?"

"He isn't well. He is healing very slowly, and the other archangels are dealing with the aftermath of demons on Earth. Only they can heal him." She patted my arm and then shut the door softly behind me.

The room was quiet and dim. In a bed in the center was my father. He wasn't hooked to any machines, but he didn't look good at all. His skin was pale, and the age lines on his face showed prominently.

Not that he had a lot of age lines to begin with.

I approached the bed and sat down in a chair. He looked so frail under the covers. I took his hand and squeezed.

"Dad?" He showed no signs of waking up. "I've seen Heaven and hell within a few days. I really need a hug right about now." I squeezed his hand and moved the chair closer. "Please be okay."

I put my head on the side of the bed, my hand still holding his. Suddenly, the gravity of the situation hit me like a ton of bricks. *I'm dead.*

My tears fell in a never-ending stream that had me turning my head into the sheet. Would this mean I could never return to my normal life again? Was my body on Earth or down in hell where it had died?

The intake in Heaven really needed to amp up their explanations.

"Please, Dad. Wake up."

A tingling sensation shot up my arm, and I sat up. With my free hand, I scrubbed the tears blurring my vision.

Oh, fuck. My hand was glowing.

My dad's eyes fluttered like they were trying to open. "Dad?"

He let out a pained moan, and his hand squeezed mine. "Healing."

"What?"

"You're healing me." His voice was raspy.

"I'm what?" My voice went up a solid octave, and I looked at our hands again. My hand was definitely glowing, but I didn't feel anything besides a slight tingle, which I thought was an effect of being dead and all. "How is that even possible? I don't know what the fuck I'm doing!"

"Language." He tried to laugh and ended up groaning instead.

I looked at my father lying in the hospital bed and choked on a sob. I had almost lost everything. I *had* lost everything. I wasn't even alive anymore.

"It's all over now." He sighed and squeezed my hand. "She can't hurt us anymore."

I looked at him and tried to control the tears swimming in my eyes. They fell anyway. "Are you-"

"I'll be fine. You should go find your boyfriends. You haven't seen them yet, have you?"

Here he was lying in a hospital bed needing his newly turned angel of a daughter to heal him, and he was worried about me seeing my four lovers.

I shook my head and looked down at my hands. "What if this changes things?"

He looked thoughtful and pushed himself up to sit against the headboard. He patted the spot next to him.

My father wasn't the most affectionate, and I stared at him blankly before he patted the bed again. I crawled onto the bed and settled in next to him. I leaned my head against his shoulder.

"Things *will* be different now. You'll have duties that you need to fulfill, but those four will always be a part of your life. Unless you don't want them to be."

"I died."

He squeezed my arm and put his cheek on top of my head. My heart squeezed in my chest. It was surprising I could still feel it beating.

We sat there in silence for several minutes before he pulled away and pulled me to look at him.

"You saved the light from the dark."

I rolled my eyes, and then we both started to laugh. It wasn't a laugh because it was funny, but a laugh because *what the fuck*. It ended with him clearing his throat.

"Are you okay?" I'd never had to ask my dad that before. He had a faraway look in his eyes.

"You're okay. That's all that matters." He put his hand on my cheek and gave me a weak smile.

I settled back into the crook of his arm. He didn't seem fine at all.

~

I MISSED Olly and Asher by half an hour. They had been released from the hospital and went back to Earth to wait for me. I had no clue where my cell phone had ended up, so it wasn't like I could call them.

It was probably lost in the depths of hell. Were there roaming charges if a demon decided to make some calls with it?

"So tell me again, how am I supposed to get back there?" I really didn't believe the woman, who had led me to the Earth entry point.

"You are making it more difficult than it needs to be. You just step off the side. Think of where you want to go. Your wings will do all the work." She was getting annoyed. I could tell from the way she pursed her lips together.

"Why aren't they coming out now? I'm telling them to."

The woman laughed and shook her head. "They will once you jump. Think of it as the maiden voyage."

"What if they don't come out?"

"They will." She let out a sigh and backed up.

"This is why new angels stay here for a while. Are you sure you don't want to stay?"

"Michael said-"

"I know. I know. He said you are an *exception* to the rule."

I let out a frustrated sigh and looked over the edge of the platform I was standing on. We were at the edge of the city, and there was a hole through the surface that looked like it fell right into an abyss of white swirling clouds.

This woman expected me to just jump and hope for the best. Could I die twice? I wasn't too keen on having my soul be lost.

"When's the next flight back?"

"There isn't. Would you prefer if I pushed you?" She had reached her limit.

"What? Hell no! I mean, sorry. Thanks for the offer."

I had my feet at the edge. Where would they be? Earth was safe now. At least as far as I knew.

I shut my eyes and stepped off.

Chapter Seventeen

Reve

I had never been one to believe that a heart could actually break. That was until blood-covered Danica had wings burst from her back. Then she flew through the stained-glass window in the ballroom, with her father in her arms.

My heart shattered right along with the window.

Toby looked at me, fear in his eyes. They seemed to ask the same questions as I was wondering. Did that mean Danica was dead?

"Go." I turned back towards the chaos that had erupted in the ballroom.

"What about you? You can't get through."

I clenched my jaw. "I have to take care of this

mess. I'll go back to Lucifer's house once I get things sorted out here."

I hoped I wasn't making a poor decision. It was possible that whoever was in charge might decide to cut Inferna off completely. If I were in charge, I would.

Inferna and Earth had no business mingling.

Toby pulled me into a hug and clapped me on the back. I pulled back and looked at him, surprised by his gesture.

"You still have piss-poor taste in sports teams." With those words, he spread his wings and flew out the window. Hopefully, he could catch up with Danica and make it through with them.

I have never been one to get overly emotional, but standing on the steps to the dais, my chosen family gone, I felt an emptiness spread throughout my body.

Shaking off the feeling, I walked up the steps and looked out across the large room where my family once hosted extravagant parties monthly.

"Enough!" I shouted, my voice naturally projecting across the room.

Hundreds of pairs of eyes landed on me, and I felt a heat moving up my neck. It had been a long time since I had to stand in front of such a large crowd.

"Lilith is dead." I looked over at the pile of ashes. That had taken some serious power to light her up like that.

The room remained silent, and then the first demon took a knee and bowed their head. I balled my hands into fists, controlling my urge to flee.

I didn't want to be King. I had never wanted the throne.

We sat at the large dining table, a feast laid before us. It was a joyous occasion for our family. I was turning half a century old, which meant my full capabilities would soon start to develop.

My father stood with his wine glass in hand. "To Reve, future King of Inferna." He looked at me at the opposite end of the table. "Son, it's time to take your place as my protege."

"Must he be so corny?" my sister, Sammy, complained from next to me.

"Samara," my mother warned from her place next to my father.

I hid my chuckle with my hand over my mouth. My younger sister was not scared of our father. She would make a great Queen if it were allowed.

We raised our glasses and drank. I gulped mine down.

"What if I don't want the throne?"

Silence fell over the room; not even a breath could be heard. My mother looked like she was going to cry. My father's face flamed red.

"Why would you reject your heritage? Your birthright?" My father's voice was dangerously low. If I didn't choose my words carefully, he was liable to snap my neck.

"Lucas is just as suitable a successor. And he wants it. I don't."

My sister shifted uncomfortably next to me. "I'll do it."

My dad made a noise in his throat. "They would kill you before you even had the crown upon your head."

I looked to my sister, who was twisting her napkin in her lap. Unlike my brother and me, she had been born with no special abilities. It was impossible for women to be dream demons since only males developed those traits. But she hadn't even developed my mother's ability to lull someone asleep with a simple touch.

"Lucas does not have the skill set required to rule. He will start a civil war among the demon races." My mother spoke quietly and then reached for her wine glass. "Your father is getting older, Reve. It is your duty as firstborn to take his place. Marry a nice demon girl. Have lots of demon babies."

I rolled my eyes. It wasn't the first time my love life had been brought to the table. I had no interest in the high-born demon girls they paraded in front of me at our monthly gatherings.

I wanted someone real. Someone to make me laugh. Someone to challenge me. Someone that wasn't afraid to be herself around me.

I looked out across the crowd of bowing forms. I found Alaric with his men, surrounding a group of other shifters that had decided it was a good idea to follow Lilith.

"Take them to the dungeons." I sounded just like my father. I had a no-nonsense edge to my voice that I hadn't known I possessed.

The room was silent as Alaric and his men led the group of demons out.

"You've freed us," a woman near the steps, still on her knee, cried out. "Long live the king!"

I *almost* laughed, but then a series of shouts repeating the phrase went up around the room. I wondered if they would still be shouting the words if they knew I was the one that killed my father and mother.

I held up my hands to signal them to stop. "I do not wish to be your king."

If there had been fans in the ballroom, the shit would have hit them. The noise hit a crescendo as the elite among the demons began talking all at once.

"Blasphemy! He can't renounce the throne!"

"There will be a civil war!"

"Where has he been all this time?"

The comments felt like a knife through my chest. These were my people. But at the same time, they weren't my people anymore.

"Quiet!" I bellowed. Jesus, I really did sound just like my father. The room fell silent. "I will meet with the Infernal Council, at least those that are present. We will decide on a plan of action. In the meantime, return to your villages and clean up the mess Lilith caused. Any demons that fought with free will for her should be handled accordingly."

With that, I turned and exited out the door behind the dais. It led to a large meeting room. Growing up, Alaric had nicknamed it "sticks" because the council members always seemed to have sticks up their asses.

I sat down at the head of the table and waited for the council members to trickle in. Many of them were familiar faces and others were new. It had been centuries upon centuries since they met in this room.

Alaric slipped in the room with three of his men, and they spread out along the perimeter. I hadn't requested his presence, but he naturally fell back into a protective role.

Once it seemed no one else was going to join the ten demons around the table, I cleared my throat and folded my hands on the table. I looked at each of them.

"Our people haven't been free in centuries. With Lilith's control over, we need to act fast to stop civil wars from breaking out among the less civilized of us."

"No offense, Your Highness, but where have you been all these years? Last I heard you were sent on a mission by Lilith to kill Lucifer and take back that section of our land."

I heard Alaric shift behind me as if to tell me he could take the council member out if I needed him to.

"It is true, I was sent to kill him. Instead, he broke the hold Lilith had over me. He gave me a choice. Die or be sent to Earth to work for him."

"And now you wish to go back to Earth?"

"Yes. My mate is there." I shut my eyes briefly to stop the tears that had suddenly felt like they were pooling somewhere behind them.

Several of the council members made noises of approval. Finding your fated mate was a big deal in Inferna.

"Who will lead us then?"

Historically, the alpha dream demon had always been King. There was no other demon that matched the capabilities and could bring all the other demons to their knees. Only the alpha had a phantom form and could push daydreams.

"We can vote, or the council can make decisions." It sounded like a good plan. Except that the democratic method wasn't even working out for Earth.

The door slammed open, and the guards moved towards the intruder.

"Get your bloody paws away from me!"

I stood and leaned against the table. My sister had fled when I told her to. Right before I killed our mother and father. I assumed she was dead or far away in the outer territories of Inferna.

"Samara?" It was somewhat of a stupid question, stemming from the shock of seeing her.

She was just like she had always been, besides her purple hair. She scrunched her nose at me and brushed her hair from her face.

"Reve, you know I hate that name." She strode

towards me and stopped. Her face softened, and then she pulled me into a hug.

"Sammy. I thought you-"

"Yeah, yeah. The rumors of angels flitting around, and the rightful king, brought me back. Word traveled fast."

I pulled back and looked at her. Wherever she had been in Inferna, she had been treated well. The guilt I felt for leaving her behind lessened.

She sat down in an empty chair, and the all-male council looked like they were about to implode. She just smiled at them.

"We are discussing serious realm business, young lady. You can wait outside." A vampire demon looked at her in disgust. "You are not welcome here with your... with your purple hair and inappropriate attire."

Sammy slowly swiveled her chair in the direction of the vampire. "You have got to be kidding me. All this time, and we still oppress women? Where I've been-"

"We know where you've been. You can go right back." The vampire was asking for it and not from me. My sister looked murderous.

I furrowed my brows and had so many questions about what my sister had been up to over the past several centuries. Now didn't seem like the appropriate time to ask.

"My people are requesting a place on the council."

Her people? I cleared my throat and took a serious look at her. Her skin seemed to glow with a power she hadn't had before. It wasn't unheard of that demons could morph into a different type of demon with time.

Lilith was an example of that if there was ever an example.

"Absolutely not!" Another man, who had been one of my father's most trusted advisors, said with a raised voice. "The gypsies are criminals! Parading around with their bright colors and debauchery!"

My sister's laugh echoed in the room. She was enjoying the drama she was causing. Or at least she was pretending she was.

"That's enough. With me stepping down, Sammy can step in for me until a solution is reached." I pushed in my chair. "Good luck."

Before they could stop me, I went phantom and left the room.

I HONESTLY DIDN'T CARE if the council bit each other's heads off. As much as I wanted to stay and catch up with my sister, I'd have to at another time.

Inferna was no longer my home. My home was where my heart was, as corny as the idea was.

Alaric was quiet most of the way back to Lucifer's territory. He had insisted he come along to protect me. I didn't need protection when I could simply vanish, but I let him accompany me anyway. Maybe he felt like he was making up for all those years ago when he left me.

"You're really going back to Earth?" He finally spoke once the iron gates of hell rose before us.

It was a vast territory of Inferna, entirely surrounded by iron bars that rose at least twenty feet in the air. Not that the gates would keep some kinds of demons out, but it would certainly keep some things in.

At first glance, it looked like a run-of-the-mill Inferna estate, but once close enough, you could sense the power behind the gates.

"I am. Once I make sure Danica is in one piece, I'll come back to see Sammy."

Alaric grunted and stopped at the main entrance of the property. There was a call box off to the side, and he pressed the button.

The gates opened immediately. Not creepy at all.

"Do you think I could come back with you?"

I stopped and turned to look at him. He had a hopeful look on his face. So did Picard, who sat on his shoulder.

"I don't get to make that decision. I'm not even sure how I'm getting back."

We walked towards the house, and Alex was waiting at the open door as if he was expecting us. A shiver ran down my spine at his gaze.

I didn't love or hate Incubus demons. We were

similar in nature. I fed off fear, and they fed off sexual desire. He seemed way too proper to be an incubus. His kind were usually outlandish and flaunted their heritage around.

"This is hell?" Alaric followed me inside and looked around. "It's just a house."

Alex laughed and led us into the kitchen. "It's underground. Would you like a tour?"

"I think I'll pass." Alaric slid onto a barstool, and Picard jumped onto the counter to sniff a pile of pastries on a plate. He dragged one off and started eating it.

"Chamuel will be up in a few minutes." Alex bowed and then left us in the kitchen.

Several minutes later, Chamuel walked into the kitchen. I was surprised the angel known for peace and love was in Inferna.

"Is Danica...?" I couldn't say it. I wouldn't say it.

"She's an angel now."

I didn't know how I felt about that. I was the odd man out now. At least with her as half-demon, I hadn't felt so alone. Would she even still want me now that she was a full-fledged angel?

It was selfish of me to even have the thoughts, considering the fact she was an angel meant she had died.

Chamuel's gaze fell on me, and his face softened. "Do not fret, son. Just because she's an angel, doesn't mean her feelings are going to change."

I nodded. I didn't feel that reassured. "Why are you here in Inferna?"

He sighed. "Things are changing. Lucifer will no longer bear this burden alone. The archangels will rotate. I volunteered to go first."

"That's very noble of you." Alaric was such a kiss-ass when he needed to be. "So, Reve and I were wondering if I could also go back to Earth."

Chamuel looked from him to Picard, then at me. He raised his eyebrows. "For what purpose? We are still tracking down demons that escaped. Why would we want to let more through?"

"I am a hunter by nature. I can help with that. I'm one of the good ones." Alaric sat up a little straighter and looked at me. "A little help here, Reve."

"He might be of use. He did help save Lucifer."

He looked at Picard, who was sitting like a meerkat, giving him puppy-dog eyes. "Very well. Let me get you back to Earth."

TIME IN HEAVEN apparently passed slowly.

When I returned from Inferna, I hadn't returned to the academy's campus. It was doubtful that would be the first place any of them would return to. Instead, I set up Alaric in my apartment and stayed at Asher's.

Toby, Asher, and Oliver returned about a week

after I had gotten home. Asher and Toby forgave me for exploding the dream I had pulled them into, on the promise that I would never go into their heads again.

The days and nights passed, and we still weren't given a date on when Danica would return. Michael said that she had a choice to stay there, plus, Lucifer was bedridden. He had drained himself almost completely of angelic power.

I didn't even know there was such a thing.

"Let's play Cards Against Humanity." Asher finished clearing off the table from dinner and grabbed us all another round of beers.

Most of our days and nights followed the same pattern. Asher went to work, Oliver went to school, Toby and I waited in case Danica returned. At night we, ate together and then played games or watched movies.

Oliver was big on learning all the games that he had no clue how to play. I was glad it wasn't his turn to pick because there was only so much of Uno and Checkers that I could take. I was pretty sure he could see through cards.

We each took seven white cards from the stack.

Asher read the first black card. "Just got dumped! Retweet #dumpedbecauseof...?"

I looked through my stack of white cards and snorted. I selected and put it face down. Oliver took the longest, staring at his very seriously. He often won because his choices made us laugh.

Asher picked the cards up and read them. "Dumped because 'jerking off into a pool of unicorn tears.' Dumped because 'Oprah.' Dumped because 'the past.' As much as I love the unicorn tears, I'm going to go with Oprah."

"Yes!" Oliver grabbed the card and did a little celebratory dance in his seat.

"Do you even know who Oprah is?" Toby took a drink of his beer and couldn't stop himself from smiling.

That's why we had game or movie night. We needed to smile. The thought of Danica never coming back or her not remembering us was too much to handle.

"Of course I know who she is."

We continued on for several more rounds until Oliver suddenly sprang from his chair, his eyes going wide and then looking at the door to the roof.

"She's back."

Chapter Eighteen

Danica

It turned out the woman who had been tasked to get me out of Heaven hadn't been wrong. As soon as I was through the opening, my wings came out of my back.

It wasn't painful like I had thought. Instead, they tingled where they connected to my back. I didn't even quite understand how two appendages so substantial could hide mysteriously inside my body.

I wasn't a believer in magic before. Now, I definitely was.

At first, everything was a foggy white as I glided down, but then land came into view. Then the city. The wings seemed to do what I wanted them to and steered me towards the old factory building in Pasadena.

I shut my eyes as my body was torpedoed towards the roof. My body righted itself, and my feet touched down gently.

"Jesus." My wings shook like a dog shaking water off after a bath and snapped away. I had at least managed to keep my eyes open most of the flight. It was easier when I was the one doing the navigating.

I looked down at my white dress and cringed. I was not a fan of dresses or the color white. It made me feel innocent.

The door leading inside burst open, and I let out a squeal of surprise. I put my hand over my heart and could feel it beating wildly.

I stood dumbstruck as Oliver stood in the doorway, a big grin on his face. I felt like I hadn't seen him in ages. Maybe I hadn't.

"Danica!" Oliver ran across the short distance and scooped me into his arms. I felt the air being squeezed out of me as he spun me around.

I was passed off to another set of arms. Asher skipped the spinning and took my face in his hands. "You remember us?" His voice shook.

I laughed and kissed him. His fingers went to my hair and pulled me closer. How scared must they have been, thinking that I had forgotten them?

"I'd never forget you." I breathed deeply, catching my breath from the spinning and kissing.

Lips brushed against my neck, and I turned

towards Tobias. He had tears in his eyes. I cupped his cheek, and he leaned into it.

"I was starting to worry you stayed there." He kissed me gently and pulled me into a hug.

Just past him, standing back from the group was Reve. His face was expressionless. Would he still want me now that I was an angel?

I pulled away from Tobias and stood in front of Reve. "Say something." I searched his eyes, hoping I could get a read on him.

"What took you so long?" He pulled me into a fierce hug that made me gasp. "Don't ever die again."

I laughed and buried my face in his shirt. I tried not to let the tears in my eyes escape. I had cried too much over the past several months. These tears were different, though. They were happy tears.

THAT NIGHT, I couldn't sleep. I shimmied out from between Olly and Tobias and made my way to the roof. I pulled the throw blanket I grabbed off the couch around my shoulders as I stepped out into the chilly November air.

I sat down on a lounge chair and stared up at the sky.

Everything in my world had changed. I was dead but was never really a human to begin with. That didn't ease the finality of what had happened.

"Can't sleep?" Reve appeared next to me and made me scoot over so he could lay next to me on his side. We barely fit on the lounger. "I can't sleep either."

I laughed and turned on my side to look at him. "What are you going to do to feed now?"

His brows furrowed together in thought. "I think I can still get into your dreams. You haven't been asleep yet, so I haven't tried." He moved hair out of my eyes. "You're my mate. Can't you feel it?"

He took my hand and put it over my chest, where my heart was beating. I shut my eyes and focused. I had always felt a pull and connection towards all four of them, but just thought it was normal when falling in love.

It had become such a normal sensation that I never gave it a second thought. I shrugged and opened my eyes.

"It feels like love. Like my heart could crack open in an instant." He brought my hand to his mouth and kissed the palm.

"Exactly." He pulled me closer and tucked me into his chest. "My father didn't have to hunt anymore once he found my mother."

I snorted back a laugh because talking about feeding off of a mate was a weird conversation. I put my ear against Reve's chest and listened to his heartbeat.

"Do you think my dad is going to be all right?"

He was still up in Heaven healing. My healing could only wake him.

"I think that your dad went through a lot. He loved that crazy bitch at one point. It's not going to be easy for him to get over something like that."

I nodded and let out a sigh.

"What else is on your mind?"

"Life. I thought I would want to be an angel, but now everything seems so final. I'm a guardian now. I could be called back to Heaven at any time. Before, when I thought I was at least half a human... I did have things I wanted out of life."

Reve stroked my back, urging me to continue.

"Like a family. One like I never had growing up. It was just my dad and me. I wanted a husband who had a big family. Maybe kids. Now though..."

He pulled away and looked at me. "You can still have all those things. With us."

I snorted. "It's illegal to marry four men. Not that we could anyways with you four not even having paperwork or whatever."

"It doesn't have to be legal. It can be just for us. As for babies... your father had you."

"But who knows how. For all we know, Lilith could have used dark magic to get pregnant." I winced at the thought of being conceived in such a way. "She used me."

He sighed and pulled me close again. "Why don't you get some sleep? It's all over now. We can finally breathe."

Chapter Nineteen

$\mathcal{I}$ stood in the empty living room of the house I had grown up in. After being released to come home, my dad decided to sell the house. He said he had bought it for Lily.

I couldn't say I blamed him. It still hurt to leave it behind.

"Are you sure you want to sell it?" I asked, turning towards him.

He had been sitting at the kitchen island, signing paperwork for the real estate agent.

"I'm sure." He stood and met me at the door. "It was a good house. At least when I was here."

We walked out the door for the last time, and he locked it behind us. "I'll see you tomorrow, bright and early?"

"Is it normal to feel nervous?" I couldn't stop the fluttering of butterflies in my stomach. Or maybe that was the tacos I had for lunch.

My dad pulled me into a hug and kissed my forehead. "I think so. I wouldn't know. I've never been married."

He unlocked his car and took off down the driveway. We had come separately because there was something I needed to do before leaving Montecito behind for good. I hadn't told my dad about it because it was against angel protocol.

I was never one for following rules.

I took one last look at the house before getting in my own car. Wings were cool and all, but I still couldn't resist driving.

I pulled up outside Ava's house and walked to the door. We still had been talking and texting occasionally, but I hadn't seen her since the night she was attacked by a vampire at Blue Wave.

She opened the door before I could even ring the doorbell. Her hair wasn't blue any longer. Now it was a dark blonde.

"What happened to your blue hair?" I walked in as she stepped out of the way, and then we hugged. "You didn't get fired, did you?"

She laughed and shook her head. "Promotion. I'm a manager now. With Kai opening the new location, he needed another manager to run the show."

"That's great, Ava!" I gave her another hug, and we sat down on the couch. "Are you still going to go to school?"

"Eventually."

An awkward silence fell over the room, and I shifted on the couch. I didn't know where to start and opened my mouth to speak several times before thinking twice.

"You're one of them. Aren't you?" She finally broke the tension. "Some kind of supernatural."

"It's a little more than that." I cleared my throat and took her hand. "You can't ever breathe a word of this."

"You know I won't. Kai explained to me that there are different types of demons after that vampire incident."

"I'm not a demon. I'm an angel." With my admission, she narrowed her eyes and then laughed. "Are you seriously laughing about me being an angel?"

"Yes. No. I don't know." She pulled her hand away and ran her fingers through her hair. "What do you mean, you're an angel?"

I gave her the short version of the past several months of my life. Her mouth was wide open by the end of it.

"You died?" Tears welled in her eyes, and I took her hand again. She looked down, and then she looked up and glared at me. "Is that a fucking engagement ring on your finger?"

I bit my lip. I should have known she would eventually notice the rock on my left ring finger. "Yes."

"Which one did you choose?" She stood and started pacing. "You aren't eloping, are you?"

I laughed. "It happened at Thanksgiving. They-"

"They? So you didn't pick one?" She stopped and looked down at me, her hands on her hips. "Isn't it against the law to have more than one husband?"

"It is. I don't quite understand why. This isn't the eighteen-hundreds. We're doing it just for us." I looked down at my hands. "I wanted you to come, but if the other angels knew that you were aware of our existence because of me. Well..."

She sighed. "You'd get in trouble."

I nodded, and she sat back down.

"I'm sorry for keeping everything from you."

"I'll get over it. You're happy, though?"

"Happier than I ever thought I could be."

"YOU JUST ABOUT READY?" my dad asked from the other side of the bathroom door.

I looked in the mirror at myself. I had gone with a simple white wedding dress that had an empire waist and flowing lace. I may not have liked white, but this day wasn't just about me. It was about four others too.

I pulled out the folded piece of paper I had shoved

in my bra. I hoped my words were enough to convey my feelings towards the four of them. I scanned it one last time and put it back in my bra. There was probably a better place to stick it, but no one would be surprised when I reached in and pulled it out.

I should have gotten a dress with pockets.

I slid open the bathroom door and smiled at my dad. "How do I look?"

His eyes glistened as he took me in. He was wearing one of his best black three-piece suits. I hadn't seen him in a suit in a long time. It was nice to see he was trying to get back to normal.

"You look beautiful." He kissed my cheek and walked me to the metal stairs leading to the roof.

My stomach was in knots. If my hands were able to sweat, they would have been. Sweat wasn't something I missed. It was quite possibly the best thing about being an angel so far.

We stopped at the top of the stairs, and he opened the door. "Ready?"

"More than ready."

There was no music. No flowers. No wedding parties. It was just Tobias, Asher, Olly, Reve, and me in front of the select few that we invited. Chamuel was officiating.

They stood at the edge of the roof in a row. My heart stuttered as we approached them dressed in their suits. I had seen Reve in a suit, but not the other three.

I was ready for our honeymoon to start immediately.

Most of the ceremony followed the standard wedding script. When we got to the vows, I pulled my folded-up piece of paper from my bra. Everyone laughed.

I cleared my throat and unfolded the paper. I had wanted to memorize what I had written but was glad I had written it down. I was an emotional mess and couldn't remember what I wrote.

"For most of my life, I've been lost. I was never really sure where I fit in. Was I an angel? Was I good enough to be an angel? Until I met you, I didn't know that being good meant more than just being perfect. Tobias, you've taught me that it means loving with your entire heart and being patient." I wiped a tear from my cheek. "Asher, you've taught me that it means not taking everything so seriously and leaning on others. Oliver, from you, I've learned that it means to let go of the past and be forgiving. And Reve, I've learned that being good means not being afraid of being different, and that keeping the darkness away means playing for the same team. Just not the Giants or the Raiders."

"Hey now." He laughed. "Those are some pretty loaded words."

I grinned. "Each of you keeps my darkness away. I can't wait to spend all of eternity with you. We might sometimes drive each other crazy, but there's no one else I'd rather go crazy with than you four."

I finally looked up then to find four pairs of eyes looking at me with all the love in the world. Maybe my words weren't the most poetic, but they were honest and how I truly felt about each of them.

Tobias spoke next. "When we first met you, none of us knew we were missing an essential part of our hearts and souls. I love that you feel so intensely and do so unapologetically. I love that you never give up and fight for what you want. I promise to protect you and love you forever."

Asher cleared his throat and pulled a card out of his pocket. I was glad I wasn't the only one that couldn't memorize a few hundred words. "I knew I was in love with you that night on the roof when you told me to stop running. I took a chance and opened my heart to you. What I got in return was a woman who allows me to breathe again. A woman who allows me to love again. A woman who makes me want to be better. I not only gained a pretty spectacular lover, but four best friends."

My dad made a coughing sound, and we all laughed.

Oliver smiled brightly at me. "I was a complete idiot when I first met you. I was lost and didn't know my purpose. But a miracle happened, and you forgave me when I wasn't sure I should be forgiven. You've opened my eyes to the world and allowed me to love with my entire heart and soul."

Hearing them say such heartfelt words to me made me want to ugly cry. Tears were already pouring down my cheeks at an alarming rate. I was a mess.

Reve stepped forward and handed me the handkerchief that was in his jacket pocket. I mouthed "thank you," and he stepped back.

"Where I'm from, they say that mates are hard to find. That only the most connected of souls will find each other during their greatest times of need. I didn't know what I was missing in my life until I found you. You saved me from a darkness that I didn't know existed in me. I walked for two thousand years without you, and it was two thousand years too long."

The ceremony came to a close, and champagne was passed around. I was giddy with excitement about going on a vacation. Alone. Just me and my four men.

"Are you going to be okay? I feel bad taking off on Christmas Eve." I hugged my dad tightly as we prepared to leave.

"I'll be fine."

"Yeah. He'll be fine." Alaric slung his arm around his shoulder. "We're going to hit Blue Wave. Pick up some fine ladies."

I rolled my eyes. "Please do not talk about my dad and picking up fine ladies in the same sentence ever again."

Picard let out a series of squeaks. It sounded like

he was laughing, but I couldn't be sure. Alaric and my father had oddly become friends over the past several weeks. Alaric had also killed a goon that had been aiming his sword at my father's head.

Asher and Olly each took one of my hands. I didn't know where we were going, but wherever it was, we'd be together.

Forever.

Epilogue

We landed on the soft sand of a beach. The sun was rising, and the sky was a gorgeous array of shades of orange. It was quiet; the only sound was the waves crashing along the shore.

Where were we? Hawaii?

"I bet you think we're in Hawaii." Tobias came behind me and slid his arms around to rest on my waist, pulling me back against him. He could never seem to keep his hands off me. It was like he thought I wasn't real and had to touch me to ensure I was there.

Now that we were married, he was never going to let me go. I wasn't complaining.

"Just because there's a beach doesn't mean I automatically assume we're in Hawaii," I lied.

He laughed and buried his face in my neck, his

beard tickling my skin. Reve stepped beside us and looked out at the waves.

"I'm still amazed at the colors in this world. Even if I have been here for centuries now." He took one of my hands and gave it a gentle squeeze.

I couldn't believe how much my life had changed in less than a year.

"YOU WANT me to put my hand where?" I looked down at the turkey in front of me. Its legs were spread wide open, and it was ready to be violated.

Tobias had to be kidding me. I knew I should have been more adamant about buying an already prepared feast. I was getting better at cooking, but not enough to want to stick my hand in a turkey's hoo-ha.

"In the cavity. It's all in a bag, Dani. All you have to do is pull it out." Tobias leaned his hip against the counter. He had an amused smirk on his face that he would pay for later.

"So, you're telling me that someone already violated this bird, put all of its guts in a bag, and then shoved it back inside? Why?" I scrunched my nose. Raw poultry gave me the willies.

"Because some people like gravy not out of a can."

I made a gagging noise. "You do it."

"I told you she wouldn't be able to do it. You owe me twenty." Reve was sitting on the end of the counter swinging his legs as he watched us fuss over the turkey.

"Can you not kick the cabinets? I'm already going to have enough to repair once I knock holes down into the units

below." Asher had just walked in from the roof where he had set up a turkey fryer.

Construction on the building would start soon, combining the three units together. We could have just moved somewhere else, but where was the fun in that?

Tobias elbowed me out of the way and took the bag of giblets out of the turkey. I cringed and went to stand between Reve's legs. He wrapped his arms around me and kissed my forehead.

"Saves the world, yet can't clean a turkey out." He laughed and slid off the counter. "You excited about your dad coming home?"

My dad had been recovering in Heaven for what felt like forever. He could have come back sooner, but he wanted to be at full health. Plus, he was supposedly creating a 'How to Guide' for running Hell since he was no longer in charge of soul redemption and torture.

Olly and I would have our turns once I was done at the academy. It wasn't something I was looking forward to.

"I am. He was wearing a suit again when I saw him last week. That's major progress."

Olly burst in through the front door, his arms weighed down by several bags. I met him halfway and took a few.

"Whose idea was it to teach Ric to drive? If I wasn't an angel, I'm pretty sure my life would have flashed before my eyes." Olly put the rest of the bags he was carrying on the table.

"You could learn how to drive." I started pulling the rest of our Thanksgiving dinner out of the bags. Apparently, it was fine to order all the sides but not the turkey.

Men.

"I don't like cars. You know that."

I wrapped my arms around his neck and stood on my tiptoes to kiss his cheek. He bent his head down and kissed me. His lips were soft as they brushed against mine. He gently pulled my bottom lip between his teeth.

"Get a room." Alaric grumbled from behind us.

"This is *our room."* I pulled away from Olly and turned toward the wolf shifter, who had become somewhat of a fixture in our lives.

We were responsible for him until my dad got back. He had volunteered to make sure he didn't get into any trouble while he was on Earth. He had saved my dad from being beheaded after all.

"Where's Picard?" Asher had an irrational fear of the little guy. Whenever Alaric was around and Picard wasn't anywhere to be seen, Asher had to know where he was. He feared a sneak attack from the monkey.

"Why? Do you miss him?" Alaric laughed. *"He's napping in the cupholder of the car."* He made himself at home and went to the refrigerator to grab himself a beer.

The door to the roof opened, and we all turned as my dad walked in, dressed in a dark gray suit and an orange tie.

I spread my wings, not caring what I knocked over, and flew up to the landing. I threw myself into his arms and he wrapped his arms around me in a tight hug.

"I see you're getting used to those wings of yours." He laughed and pulled back to look at me. *"You look beautiful."*

Tears stung my eyes, and I swallowed the lump in my

throat. I still randomly burst into tears thinking about all that had transpired.

"Thank you. You're looking pretty good yourself."

We joined the others, and hugs and handshakes were exchanged.

"Alaric." My dad stuck out his hand. "Thank you."

They shook firmly before Alaric pulled him into a hug and slapped his back like they had known each other for their entire lives.

Once dinner was ready, we all headed to the roof where the guys had set up a large table. Lights were strung up all around the rooftop, and there were a few patio heaters set up near the table.

My heart felt like it would burst as we all gathered around. Thanksgiving was usually just my dad and me, but now my family had grown.

The basket of rolls was handed my way, and I folded back the cloth napkin that was covering them. My breath caught in my throat.

I must have stared in the basket for a solid minute as everyone at the table sat silently watching me. I finally reached in and took out the small velvet box.

I flipped the box open and brought my hand to my mouth to stop myself from making an embarrassing sound. The ring was beautiful, with one large diamond surrounded by four smaller diamonds.

"Will you marry us?" Olly turned toward me and took my hand. "We love you and want you to have everything you've ever wanted."

I looked at each of their hopeful faces as tears slid down my cheeks. I was completely caught off guard.

I looked at my dad, who I swore swiped at his eye. He gave me a slight nod of the head. Not that I would have changed my mind had he shaken it.

"Yes." A laugh burst out of me, the same way you see in the movies. I inwardly cringed and swore to never make fun of women's reactions at proposals again.

Olly grinned and slid the ring onto my finger.

I SMILED at the memory of how they had asked me to marry them. There had definitely been a lot of shitty moments in the past several months, but the last month made up for those tenfold.

"Are you going to tell me where we are?" It had been the middle of the day back in California. We were clearly somewhere on the other side of the world.

"We are near Fuck It, Thailand." Olly kicked his dress shoes off and peeled his socks off his feet.

"We've told you a million times, angel baby, it's Phuket." Asher laughed and put his arm around Olly's neck, yanking him to his side. "There will be a lot of fucking going on, though."

"This is a private island. It's a wedding gift from your dad." Tobias unwrapped himself from around me and took my other hand.

I followed them down the shoreline and then away from the shore to the stretch of large trees.

"Where are we staying?" I hadn't seen a house when we landed.

Hands covered my eyes, and I nearly tripped over my feet. They laughed, and we continued walking.

"You guys aren't going to kill me, are you?" Laughter filled my ears.

We stopped, and the hands left my eyes.

It took a minute for my brain to process what I was seeing. Up in the trees, half-hidden, was the largest treehouse I had ever seen.

There was a large wraparound deck that had blue Christmas lights strung around the railing and large picturesque windows on all sides. One window had a Christmas tree standing in front of it, the white lights twinkling.

I brought my hand to my mouth and couldn't stop the tears from flowing. These men had turned me into a crier.

Olly scooped me up into his arms and carried me toward the wooden stairs. They wound their way around the base of one of the trees and up onto the deck.

"Asher designed this." Olly slid open the door and walked inside the house. He put me down, and I took in the room.

The living room was large, with sliding windows on two walls. The sleek, white kitchen was open to the living room, which was decorated in blues. I really couldn't wait to see where we'd be sleeping.

My guess was the stairs leading up to another level was where the bed was.

"It's gorgeous." I turned back toward my guys standing in front of the tree.

I could think of no better way to spend my Christmas than with four men who looked at me like I was their entire world. I hoped they knew they were my entire world too.

Other Books by Maya Nicole

Celestial Academy

Ascend

Descend

Transcend

Standalones

Widow

Infernal Council

Infuse

Defuse

Transfuse

Salinity Cove

Surge

Social Media

Be sure to join my Facebook group or social media for book release updates.
https://www.facebook.com/groups/mayanicoleauthor/

Instagram @mayanicoleauthor

Twitter @MayaAuthor

Made in the USA
Monee, IL
13 July 2020